A CBC Best Canadian Fiction of 2018 Selection

A Toronto Star Best Book of the Year

An NPR Best Book

Finalist for the 2019 Amazon Canada
First Novel Award

Finalist for the 2019 Kobo Emerging
Writer Prize in Literary Fiction

Finalist for an Audie Award

SCOTIABANK GILLER PRIZE
25
LONGLIST

"[*Split Tooth*] boldly and cohesively mixes memoir,
traditional folk tales, poetry and fiction to depict the
humiliations and hilarities of coming-of-age, the formidable
power of Nunavut's landscape, the resilience of women. . . .
[The book is] exhilarating in its carnality, experimentation,
vulnerability and wisdom." NOW MAGAZINE

"Tagaq's surreal meld of poetry and prose transmutes the
Arctic's boundless beauty, intensity, and desolation into a
wrenching contemporary mythology." THE NEW YORKER

D1016685

More praise for

SPLIT TOOTH

"What Tagaq offers with *Split Tooth* is a still too rare glimpse
of the inner lives of young people, particularly girls and women,
living in northern and rural communities. . . . Tagaq's music
is intensely corporeal and so is her writing. . . . [Her] emotional
intelligence is aspirational."

—Anupa Mistry, *The Globe and Mail*

"Neither fully autobiography nor fiction, *Split Tooth* is brutal,
beautiful literary magic."   —*Exclaim!* magazine

"An ambitious and acrobatic blend of memoir, fiction, poetry,
and dream journals."   —*Refinery29*

"Tanya's book is one of the most incredible things I've ever
read. It's deeply profound, emotional and personal, and furthers
her artistic experimentation and genius into a new realm.
I love her even more after reading it, and I'm once again awed
by her talent."   —Jesse Wente, CBC Radio

"Tagaq's genre-defying work establishes her as a careful, gifted
wordsmith."   —*Publishers Weekly*

S P L I T

T A N Y A

TOOTH

TAGAQ

PENGUIN

an imprint of Penguin Canada, a division of Penguin Random House Canada Limited

Penguin Canada
320 Front Street West, Suite 1400, Toronto, Ontario M5V 3B6, Canada

Originally published in hardcover by Viking Canada,
a division of Penguin Random House Canada Limited, in 2018.

Published in this edition, 2019

1 2 3 4 5 6 7 8 9 10

Library and Archives Canada Cataloguing in Publication data is available upon request.

ISBN 978-0-14-319805-5
eBook ISBN 978-0-14-319804-8

Cover and interior design: Jennifer Griffiths
Cover image and interior illustrations: Jaime Hernandez
Inuktitut translation: Julia Demcheson

Printed and bound in Canada

www.penguinrandomhouse.ca

Penguin
Random House
PENGUIN CANADA

For the Missing and Murdered Indigenous Women and Girls,
and survivors of residential schools.

"What is a poet? An unhappy man who hides deep anguish
in his heart, but whose lips are so formed that when the sigh
and cry pass through them, it sounds like lovely music. . . .
And people flock around the poet and say: 'Sing again soon'—
that is, 'May new sufferings torment your soul but your lips
be fashioned as before, for the cry would only frighten us,
but the music, that is blissful.'"

SØREN KIERKEGAARD, *Either/Or*

SPLIT
TOOTH

1975

Sometimes we would hide in the closet when the drunks
came home from the bar. Knee to knee, we would sit, hiding,
hoping nobody would discover us. Every time it was different.
Sometimes there was only thumping, screaming, moans,
laughter. Sometimes the old woman would come in and
smother us with her suffering love. Her love so strong and
heavy it seemed a burden. Even then I knew that love could
be a curse. Her love for us made her cry. The past became a
river that was released by her eyes. The poison of alcohol on
her breath would fill the room. She would wail and grab at us,
kissing us, kissing the only things she could trust.

Fake-wood panel walls, the smell of smoke and fish. Velvet
art hung on the walls, usually of Elvis or Jesus, but also polar
bears and Eskimos.

The drunks came home rowdier than usual one night,
so we opted for the closet. We giggle nervously as the yelling
begins. Become silent when the thumping starts. The whole
house shakes. Women are screaming, but that sound is

overtaken by the sound of things breaking. Wet sounds of flesh breaking and dry sounds of wood snapping, or is that bone?

Silence.

There are loud pounding footsteps. Fuck! Someone is coming towards us. We stop breathing. Our eyes large in the darkness, we huddle and shiver and hope for the best. There is someone standing right outside the closet door, panting.

The door slides open, and my uncle sticks his head in. Towering over us, swaying and slurring. Blood pouring down his face from some wound above his hairline.

"I just wanted to tell you kids not to be scared."

Then he closed the door.

It's 9 a.m., late for school

Grade five is hard

Rushing, stumbling to get my pants on

Forgetting to brush my teeth

Dreading recess

The boys chase us and hold us down

Touch our pussies and nonexistent boobs

I want to be liked

I guess I must like it

We head back to class

The teacher squirming his fingers under my panties

Under the desk

He looks around and pretends he's not doing it

I pretend he's not doing it

He goes to the next girl and I feel a flash of jealousy

The air gets thinner and tastes like rot

School is over

I leave for the arcade

Watch out for the old walrus

The old man likes to touch young pussy

We try to stay away

I wonder why nobody kicks him out

Things are better at home now

Three's Company and a calm air
Archie comics and Lego
Goodnight

Smells unleashed from the spring thaw lift us into a frenzied desperation for movement. The air is so clean you can smell the difference between smooth rock and jagged. You can smell water running over shale.

Lichen smells sweet. The green lichen smells different from black. In the spring you smell last fall's death and this year's growth, as the elder lichen shows the young how to grow.

The freeze traps life and stops time. The thaw releases it. We can smell the footprints of last fall and the new decomposition of all who perished in the grips of winter. Global warming will release the deeper smells and coax stories out of the permafrost. Who knows what memories lie deep in the ice? Who knows what curses? Earth's whispers released back into the atmosphere can only wreak havoc.

Sprigs of green begin to push their shy lives through the ice blanket. The songs of migratory birds are like alarms that awaken us from the torpor of winter. Life has arrived! The ice begrudgingly recedes, promising vengeance in a few short weeks. Winter always wins. The sun scoffs. Nothing can stop the cacophony of gluttony and procreation about to ensue.

The sea ice is still strong, but the ponds have melted and are now open. The mosquito larvae swirl in their figure eights, hypnotizing and beautiful. A stark contrast to what they will be in a few days, when their metamorphosis turns them into the cyclone of bloodthirst. I am certain that if I ever had the opportunity to torture an enemy, they would find themselves naked on the tundra in mosquito season, with their hands tied behind their back.

As children in spring, we have the run of the town. Just as we have grown weary of our parents' company, they have been tolerating our frenetic housebound antics for half a year. The twenty-four-hour sun is feeding our visions and keeping us warm. We run the dusty streets looking for adventure. Large gangs of kids and large packs of loose dogs roam the town. I wonder which group is more rabid. None of my friends have curfew, but I do. We must get our adventure done before eleven!

We leave town and come upon a smallish pond. It's about fifty metres long, half as wide. There are blue Styrofoam pieces lying around, wind-blown from construction sites from the last building season. We decide to play hero and use the flimsy pieces of Styrofoam as boats. Considerations like the high winds, the near-zero temperature, and the depth of the pond are carried away like bits of Styrofoam. These things never occur to eleven-year-olds.

No one knows how to swim. We take turns paddling out with sticks as paddles, our little bodies balancing precariously on our wobbling blue vessels. The wind picks up. One of us inevitably gets blown out too far, his makeshift paddle grossly inadequate to get him back to shore. He is the smallest of the group. He always was. Meek, quiet, and always smiling. No wolves picked on him because he was so good-natured. He was the prettiest of the boys, and the girls carried either a maternal instinct or a quiet crush on him. We kissed once; his mouth small and soft, his tongue slow.

The wind pushes him out deeper. If he falls in, he will drown. Everyone knows this. Nobody speaks. We let the wind do the howling, as his little face grows worried. He is in the middle of the pond now. His thin windbreaker is flapping up against him, revealing protruding ribs and a slight shiver. I can see his slightness, sense his vulnerability. The only sound is the wind and the flapping fabric of our clothing. His face becomes perfectly calm, more calm than normal. He looks like a serene old man; he looks like everything is all right. The wind gusts and the Styrofoam tips to one side, and then the other. But his body knows what to do. I see him take a deep breath, and his breath steadies his ride. He is close to the far side now. I see his hands shake as he dips his stick back into the water. He is safe. He has reached the other side. His eyes look more grown up. We have witnessed him become a man. We all cheer! It is past eleven; I rush home.

We made it our Styrofoam game. The next week, seven kids drowned in a larger pond closer to the airport after using a water tank cut in half as a boat. We never played our Styrofoam game again.

Inhale small fears they turn into doubts into words into ideas into anger into hatred into violence.

Exhale large fears and large words they tumble back onto you it's easy to get buried by our own mirrors.

Inhale small fears and they whisper and travel to your mind observe them and thank them for trying to protect you.

Exhale acknowledgment of the beauty within your instincts and the courage to love small fears.

Inhale hard love suck in the smell and reward reap eat chew swallow devour all the goodness and love that is given to you.

Exhale calmness in acknowledgment of the beauty within the courage it takes to not fear love.

It's a dusty summer night in the High Arctic. The sun is shining brightly overhead. The sun always brings life and mischief, serenity and visions. It's two o'clock in the morning and I've shrugged off my curfew. There will be hell to pay when I get home and my father's thunderous footsteps shake the house with a blazing ire that only he can conjure.

It's worth it to disobey and join my brethren in our celebration of freedom, electricity, and curiosity. Fingertips anxious and knock knees oscillating, we conjure and conspire; we harness desires and swat away doubt. The winter was long and oppressive. We all knew that soon we would be in our teenaged years and this time was precious. All children on the cusp of puberty seem to understand that this magic time will end soon. Greeting the future and yearning for maturity and yet planted firmly in the moon. Revelling in our youth, wishing it would never end. Never seeing past the tips of our noses as we are driven through our bodies with the perfect lightning strike of growing cells and perceived immortality.

We transcend time and pluck smiles off each other's faces. Dig giggles out of rib cages and shoot insults as if they were compliments.

There is a siren that sounds in our small town to announce the curfew. At noon and at 10 p.m. Every time the siren sounds all the sled dogs howl, and I imagine that they think there is a large, loud god dog that rules the land howling. I equate this with religion. A short-sighted and desperate attempt for humans to create reason and order in a universe we can't possibly comprehend. The simple truth is we are simply an expression of the energy of the sun. We are the glorious manifestation of the power of the universe. We are the fingertips of the force that drives the stars, so do your job and FEEL.

Our black-haired human pack has decided to hang out by the steps behind the school. Our gnashing teeth and gums hungry for activity, tongues generating conflict and imaginary realities where we were interesting and relevant, not just kids on the school steps. Not part of this boring old town of twelve hundred souls (if you only count the humans, but whoever said only humans can have the universe living in them?). The back steps are a less conspicuous choice than the front because the summer sun reveals all to prying eyes. There is a large water tank by the back steps; this is good. We can use it to hide behind if we hear the bylaw truck. This is one of our favourite games, hiding from the bylaw enforcement officer. His job is to drive around town and chase the kids home and shoot stray dogs. He wants us to be safe in bed. Are beds safe anyways?

Brightness. Laughter. We are a gangly group of five girls and one small boy. We are stuck in the horrid torrent of awkward crushes and curious sideways glances. Clumsy advances with no goal other than to say someone liked you. The time of wistfully watching the teenagers French kiss by the jukebox and hoping one day we would be free to say yes. In those days I didn't even know how to say no.

All I had was my speed and agility. Alas the boys have just recently gotten faster, stronger, and taller than I and it breaks me because I used to be the best. My ego is in a state of flux. I am powerless now and have lost my flagpole in our social setting. I was the fastest. It's a tough pill to swallow for a tomboy. I miss being able to beat the boys. I used to be a ball-kicker. The one boy hanging out with us this evening is a little younger than the rest of us; cocksure, and small for his age. His skin is dark brown and his eyes so black. I love the way his hair is so black that it shines blue in the sun. He is so very cute, yet his voice has not cracked yet, his balls haven't dropped. The girls want to hold him like a doll. But he's a dick, the way only insecure people can be a dick. He annoys me in a lot of ways, but nothing needles me more than the way he makes fun of me for having a crush on my friend. She doesn't know it, so the boy's adolescent judgment leaves me

embittered and confrontational. I've always loved girls, and our insufferable town sees this love as deviance. This little shithead is not helping.

We are picking up stale old cigarette butts and smoking the last puffs off them, burning our lips and fingers on the indignity of it all. There are always plenty of butts around the Bay or the Co-op, but we have exhausted the supply tonight. The high school kids usually smoke around these back steps, so we find some good long ones because the kids have to throw them away when the teachers try to sneak up and catch them red-handed.

The little boy is in a taunting mood. He is yapping about how boys are just better than girls. Boys are stronger, boys are faster, and boys are smarter. Faggots are disgusting and he hates them. He looks like a mosquito to me. I have an idea. I jump down from my perch on the railing and grab him from behind. He is so slight. I wrestle him easily to the ground and tell the others to help me. We are laughing hysterically. I peel off his shirt. His little brown tummy is so taut. Wiry little six-pack, skinny little arms. We take off his pants too. His ankles are so thin. He is so delicate. He has large black moles peppered on his dark skin. He smells like smoke and panic. He has no hair yet. Two girls hold his legs, one his arms, and I'm pulling his clothes off. It's our turn to be mean.

He is yelling for us to quit it, but we are tickling him, so he is also laughing uncontrollably. We leave his underwear and socks alone for dignity's sake and take his pants and shirt. We run as fast as we can towards Main Street with our bounty as he follows, screaming for us to return his clothing. As we turn the corner onto Main, we see other groups of kids. I assume that he won't dare be seen unclothed, but he bravely turns the corner and simply throws the other group a toothy smile and keeps sprinting. Gasping breaths and burning lungs, thighs aflame; we let the world own us. Soles flying and hearts pounding, we turn the next corner and see a group of adults. Gleefully squealing, we keep going knowing he will not pursue. He won't risk being seen by adults.

I think of all the times I have been told I was inferior for being a girl. I think about all the times men have touched me when I didn't want them to. I think about how good it feels to be waving the pants of one of the cocky boys in the air while he hides behind the corner. We keep running and circle the school. He is waiting for us on the other side, swatting mosquitoes and crying. This is not the last time he will get himself into trouble with bravado that cannot be backed up. He ends up dying that way.

STERNUM

The Human Sternum is capable of so many things
Protector of Diaphragm
Killer and milk feeder of hope
Marriage of marrow and cartilage
Heaving
Imprisoning the heart
Keeps it alive
Cage for Blood and breath
The Human Sternum is used for so many things
Clavicles like handlebars
Ribs like stairs
The sternum is the shield
Even when impaired
Even when it smothers a little girl's face
As the bedsprings squeak

There is a small bog on the tundra about three minutes outside of town. The bog is littered with pieces of plywood blown by the fierce Arctic winds from various construction sites. The mighty winter winds and the permafrost leave only a few months for building. The construction crews work twenty-four hours a day under the midnight sun. Chasing a few pieces of plywood that have been carried off by the High Arctic winds is not a good reason to put down your tools.

Under those pieces of plywood is shelter from the wind for a myriad of species. The plywood becomes home in the vast treelessness. The wood becomes a dark sanctuary safe from all the predators. We find creatures underneath the plywood, from beetles and baby birds to lemmings. The lemmings are my favourite. They get so startled as I rip off the ceiling from their safety, blindly running to find escape from this monster that has changed their world.

After chasing and capturing them I hold each one in my cupped hands, singing to it until its heartbeat returns to normal cadence. I put them in my pockets. Don't put more than one in each pocket or they will start fighting. Not many creatures are good in overpopulated spaces. I have about six pockets in my windbreaker. Six lemmings a day keeps the doctor away.

Whistling my way home and brimming with anticipation for my daily ritual; I have only five lemmings today. There is a small back porch in our house. Since nobody ever uses the back door, the porch is my domain. It's a good place to hide things, a good place to pretend the rest of the world is mine. Stopping at the fridge to pick out a few carrots and some celery, I then lay the lemmings out on the floor of the bare porch. The carrots belong in the corner. The animals are afraid at first, but cannot resist the smorgasbord of food. I leave them happily munching and starting to relax.

We have a fish tank in our living room. There are newts, snails, and fish in there. The snails procreate too quickly for the health of the tank, so my ritual begins by killing off a minimum of ten snails by simply squishing their little bodies against the glass, shells and all. It is very satisfying to me to hear their shells popping, like when you find a particularly dirty part on the rug while you are vacuuming, and it all clinks up the tube in a hollow symphony.

Part two of my ritual is to take one of the newts by the tail and put it into my mouth. It sits there on my tongue, the little suction cups on its toes grasping my taste buds. I close my mouth. It crawls around in confusion for a minute, and then finds comfort in the heat and darkness. It squirms its way under my tongue, and usually falls asleep there. I do some chores as it rests, opening my mouth to let some fresh air in. I go and look into the bathroom mirror. The newt is almost always sleeping, its cute little eyes closed and restful, using my tongue as a huge duvet. I find it adorable. I return him to the tank, and go to find my furry friends.

The lemmings are fed and full. I lie down in the small porch. I can fit lengthwise in the porch if my knees are bent. I fan out my long hair on the floor and wait. I lie still. The lemmings calm, and begin to stir. They find my hair. This awakens their burrowing instinct. They make their way to my scalp, seeking safety. The smallest of paws massaging my head at lightning speed. They never leave the safety of my hair. They keep going for about ten minutes before they get weary of attempting to dig. It's the best ten minutes of my day. It's still the best massage I have ever gotten. Once they tire, I put them back into my pockets and return them to where I found them. I have to get them out before my parents come home. The lemmings are full of carrots and happy. I will come back tomorrow. My mother once found one small piece of lemming poop in my hair. She laughed so hard and wondered how it got in there. I told her I was lying down on the tundra. I have kept this small ritual to myself until now.

"Just let me get it wet" he said

What does he mean?

It's not wet down there

I didn't even have hair yet

I lie wooden

Saying no

He keeps trying

Pushing his hard thing

Into a space that has no space

It's dry

The heaving desperation on his breath

The sour fear on mine

Finally someone comes to the door

And he jumps off me

Pretending like nothing happened

NINE MILE LAKE

My little cousin, you were only seven years old. I was eleven, the big girl. We pilfered money from our parents and went to the store. The Resolute Bay Co-op always had a particular smell. It smelled dry, a little like mildew and a lot like dust. The aisles seemed so long to our small bodies. After intense negotiation of what to buy, we left with two giant plastic bags of junk food. Cokes, M&M's, salt and vinegar potato chips, the weird pink popcorn with an elephant on the package, Popeye cigarettes, and even a few real cigarettes.

We lit the cigarettes behind the old A-frame house near the playground, hoping that our mothers would not see us. We had already been caught smoking under the porch while eating a bottle of Flintstones vitamins earlier that summer. Nobody was happy with us on that day. I was aware of being the bad influence, but I could never keep you from following me from place to place. Sometimes I would trick you and run away, and then feel bad and come back, your little tear-stained face making me feel like I had no soul. I never let you tag along while hanging out with the big boys, because we were always up to no good. You were too small for all of that chaos. I did my best to protect you. I still do.

It was getting late, but it didn't matter. The twenty-four-hour sun was blazing high in the sky, and the cold wind kept us alert. Three months of bright light meant that there was no curfew, no time constraints. We wanted an adventure, which usually meant a hike out of town. There were a few interesting places we could go on our trek, considering the vastness of the tundra. The river was relatively close, where we would balance a two-by-four between the jagged rocks of the rapids and cross, praying our makeshift bridge would not falter. We could go to the beach. The shore was ripe with seaweed and their treasures. Remember that time we found a sea snake, its bloated corpse so cold and lonely? The playground was all right, but inevitably one particular gas-sniffing jerk would come along and pester us. Best to get out of town.

We marched out on our own, feeling like big girls, teen-aged girls. You trailed behind on your tiny legs. We headed for Signal Hill. Making it to the transmission tower was good, but I wanted the cliffs. It was a steep climb and our breath was heavy when we reached the top. We ate half of our food as we sat on the summit, our feet dangling over the precipice as we kept our eye out for polar bears. My uncle used to slide down this hill in the winter. I remember thinking that he was the coolest, and hoped I would be brave enough take risks like him when I grew up.

We decided to try to make it to Nine Mile Lake. It seemed like just a few kilometres from the top of the hill. This is when I learned that on the tundra, everything is much farther than it seems. The treeless expanse lends itself to illusion. We could handle it. The most daunting task was passing the seagulls' nests. There was no going around them; we had to run through their nesting zone. Courage does not come easily, and we run as quickly as possible, your little hand in mine.

Seagulls scream and dive when you get near their nests. I held my fist up into the sky and waved it as we ran, so they would go for the highest point of contact. I could feel their beaks pecking through my thin glove. We ran as quickly as we could, even losing a few bags of chips from our precious rations. We were red-faced and laughing once we made it through. I will never forget your sweet little face that day, proud and exhilarated with our accomplishment. I carried your heart in mine. I still do.

The tundra is sparse, rocky, no trees and hardly any dirt. The lichen takes hundreds of years to grow. They grow and die and eventually collect to make up the soil. We were surrounded by shale rock, dry and sharp under the feet. The clean and hollow crackle of walking on shale is still one of my favourite sounds.

We lifted a piece of plywood and found a snow bunting's nest under it. Three bald baby birds screamed at us. They were so small, newly hatched. The veins under their still-closed eyelids were purple and throbbing, their necks barely strong enough to hold up their heads. Shrill cries filled the air, and a panic arose. We wanted to make them happy! Were they hungry? We opened up the elephant popcorn. We fed the little mouths. In horror, we watched as each one of them choked on the popcorn and died. We could see the kernels through their little transparent throats. There was nothing we could do. The mother came back from her insect hunt and made us cry even harder. We left in defeat, feeling like demons and hoping neither of us would speak of it again. I made the biggest mistakes with you. I still do.

Finally arriving at Nine Mile Lake, we were thankful that the wind had died down a bit. We were relieved because polar bears can't smell you as easily. The water was vast and clean. Thirst is easily quenched by fresh Arctic water. Around the periphery of the lake, there were small pools that held baby trout. I trapped one and put it in my mouth. I let it swim down my esophagus; its tail tickled all the way down to my tummy. It was delightful. The flesh was so fresh. Something awoke in me, an old memory; an ancient memory, of eating live flesh. It is a true joining of flesh to flesh. My spine straightened. When flesh is eaten live, you glean the spirit with the energy. That is why wild predators are so strong.

The farther away you get from the time of death, the less energy meat carries. We pretended to be seagulls, not even chewing the fish and feeling them swim down our throats. We gorged ourselves on them. The energy of the fish's life was readily absorbed into my body, and its death throes became a shining and swimming beacon into the sky. If we acted like seagulls, then perhaps we could transform into them, screaming and soaring. We would fly home.

THE TOPOGRAPHY OF PITY

Look at other humans with pity.

Why are they so downtrodden?

What could possibly have happened to them?

What could possibly have happened to you?

They may see the consumer sickness

They may see the pride sickness

They may see the detachment sickness

Your belongings won't save you

Money won't save you, even if you save it

Money has spent us, as we have spent it

We look upon the scarred earth with pity

What have we done to her?

Isn't it she who has given her minerals

And electricity

To spit us out,

Give us life?

Only to suck us back in

Just so she can breathe with the seasons?

Just so we can be her topsoil?

Perhaps she looks upon us not with the love of a mother

But with the same indifference we lend to our lungs

With the same indifference

That we give the homeless human

THE FIRST TIME IT HAPPENED

Only children rule this house. On a cold summer night we gather. There is tinfoil on the windows to keep the sun out, socks stuffed into the hole where the doorknob should be to prevent the smaller kids from spying on us. We are in a safe house, where nobody is drinking. No adults, our rules.

There are six or seven of us, just hanging out with our imaginations and our ideals. Everything is so simple. We live second by second. I am eleven. Some kids start playing tag, running and screeching with joy. Three of us are sitting on the bare mattress, backs against the wall and our backs to the world. A Blondie cassette tape is playing over and over. The older kids boss the younger ones around, teasingly telling them to respect their elders. We spin the bottles and hide the seek. We have lip-syncing competitions and raid the kitchen shelves. We get peanut butter in our hair and bark laughter over nothing. We have been awake for so long that sweet humorous delirium has set in. Someone farts and we all laugh for fifteen minutes straight. Someone shoots Kool-Aid out of his nose in a fit of hilarity and a huge booger came along with it and we laugh so hard and long that it hurt.

I feel something enter the room, coming in from the top right corner. I cannot see it but I know it's there, plain as day. My real self recognizes the feeling, recognizes the place this being came from, where it lives. There are other realities that exist besides our own; it is foolish to think otherwise. The universe is conscious. This thing comes from the layers of energy beyond our physical perception. The place we go to after we die, the place we were before being conceived. These places hold us for millennia in Universe Time. We are on Earth and in flesh for only a moment. Before we are born, energy must be woven into spirit and then siphoned into a body. After we die the spirit must be consoled after the trauma of flesh and then unravelled back into energy. It feels good to remember this place, but the thing that has arrived here is not good.

It is terrifying to feel this being so clearly. If it were a sound, it would be a quiet one that got louder until it is the only thing that you can think about. Warning crawls all over me. This thing grows and reveals its intent. This thing is not done with the flesh; it wants to get inside mine. It feels like a squirming, penetrating, living giant, pushing and crushing at the boundaries of my skin. It's looking for cracks, holes, pores, any way into the flesh. I'm curious and wonder what would happen if I let it in. I wonder what the process of letting it in would be. I am not afraid, only curious. I don't feel like prey. I too am a predator.

Time is standing still; there are minutes between each clock tick. I realize that not everyone can feel the being, because nobody else is agitated. My cousin's eyes meet mine in the slow stop time. She can feel it too! She is sitting cross-legged on the mattress, facing me. We both instinctively know what to do. Where did the knowledge come from? No one has taught us how to do this, but the ritual is old and living in our bones. Just as giving birth is involuntary, we fall into rank to facilitate a process we don't comprehend yet. She bends over and rests her head on my lap, and I feel a click in the unphysical place, like two puzzle pieces snapping together. She pushes her energy into mine, and we become one being Ourselves. She is the intent that moves the hand. I am the door. She is a battery, she provides the torque; I am the beacon, calling and igniting the energy that creates the path to crack this reality. There is a great snap, like a spine breaking.

It's the strangest sensation being in this New Place. I can hear everything, but it is muffled, as if I am hearing it through a small tube filled with cotton batting. Everything around me is devoid of light and I am weightless. There is freedom and relief from conscious troubles. I am not in my body. Time has changed into a light and benign thing, because it is no longer ripping through my physical form.

31

SPLIT TOOTH

It is Time that eats us and drives us back into the earth. Without a body, things like Time and Gravity have no power.

After what seemed like an eternity of easing into and spreading myself out in this New Place, I sense slight movement to the right of me. It's a small stirring movement about three feet away. There are two bright almond-shaped holes floating at what would have been my eye level. Light is coming out of them like how a television glows in a dark room. I can see children running around the room my body was in through those almond-shaped holes; I can see the threadbare blankets on the mattress. I can see the reality of my body. Those are my body's eyes I am looking through.

The realization doesn't startle me, because the comfort of being outside of Body is our true state of existence. The calmness turns into slow dread as I feel the presence of the being that entered the room earlier. I can see what this thing is, now that I have left my body.

It is very sharp, gnarled, masculine, canine, long-toothed and rotted. It was a human once. It is huge and sinuous, a jumble of muscle and gristle. It has no skin in most places, and was blinded by cataracts and hatred. I could sense he had died in a terrible way, possibly more than once. He has honed the echo of the burden of revenge. He is murderous. I feel him, and he is bitter. He wants to come back to physical form because something terrible needs to be avenged. I know it is because of an act of evil that he died. He is lightning quick and slobbering. One of the children in the room is related to someone he wants to wreak revenge upon. He wants to kill the child, and anyone else he can. The killing will give him skin, sight, honour, and release some of the hatred. It will heal his family's DNA; it will bring good fortune to his living brethren. It will restore balance. Murder can heal if applied sparingly. Murder can feed us. Life murders us every day.

The being is now up in the left-hand corner of the room, and then suddenly it is rushing towards me, towards the light. It's fast, so fast I can hardly see it. He is rushing towards the eyeholes. He must place his own consciousness onto my body's eyeholes to claim my flesh. Once he presses his face onto my body's eyes, they will be his. I know if he manages to claim my eyes, my whole body will be his. He is directly beside my spirit self now, rushing towards my flesh, his new reality just a moment away. I can't believe his power, his clear beauty, and his hatred. It is the sharpest thing I have ever sensed.

At the very last second I awaken out of the trance and use all of my will to push him away and jump into my own field of vision. Moving him was like shoving a wet, seething mountain. It burns to make contact with him. It took my last reserve of mental and spiritual strength to push him away. I place my eyes onto the eyeholes for the Bonding. It feels like blue light is being poured onto my face, and Body feels like a million pounds of dark matter. I can feel Time again, and it feels like death. It's excruciating. As spirit fastens itself totally back into flesh, there is another great snapping sound, and an electrical current goes through me.

The only physical sign of this is a slight twitch in my arms. All of the kids in the room scream in horror when I move. It must have been an unnatural movement because the boy beside me hides behind a pillow and starts to cry. A few more children run out of the room. Even though there had been no previous indication that anything was amiss, the children instinctively know to flee. I'm in a deep daze. My cousin looks up at me as if in a dream, and we both break out in wicked grins. She was with me that whole time. She saw. It was nice to harness the fear.

Something is lurking
Something sideways
Something hollow
Something pasty and shallow
Something jittery
Something slow
Sucking on mud and
Filled with woe

Something is stirring
Something full
Something thick and cold
Something imperceptible
Something unseen
Something war-driven
Something obscene

It makes me want to hide in blankets and make bad choices
It makes me want to destroy what's in front of me
It can be freed only with tears

1978

It's early morning. The Frosted Flakes have grown soggy. I'm stuck staring at one of the half-submerged flakes, half crispy, half mushy. Tap tap tap the spoon against the ceramic bowl; it seems to help shake off the sleep that refuses to lift from the top of my head. It feels fuzzy and numb. Boredom hang-over. It's pitch-black outside. Dead winter. We have not seen the sun in months. Stars stare at me through the window. Wind screams urgently, shaking the house. Wind sings but carries an axe instead of a note.

A dog howls. Five more follow suit. I put on my kamiit and kick the door open because it has frozen shut. School has not been cancelled: it's not cold enough outside. It has to be at least minus fifty with the wind chill to merit a day off. The roads are frozen solid; they will stay that way until May or June.

The permafrost is living under everything, slowing time and preserving what would normally rot. Kamiit help feet deftly navigate the slip of the ice, the crunch of the snow, and the depths of the drifts. The sealskin is warm, but I have lost the blood my feet carry. The Cold has scared the blood out of my toes. Our feet have built-in memory of which tendons to curl to prevent falling on all different kinds of ice. The Snow would sometimes slice the surface of the ice in half with a drift, and try to trick us into falling. The Snow could crunch underfoot or chase you loosely. The Snow could hold your whole body weight or decide to deceive you and plunge you into the down underneath.

Snow is fickle. Snow picks itself up and goes wherever Wind tells it to. One element controls the other in a cyclical oblivion. Weather is just the earth's breaths. Wind is the cold bearer and the death bringer. Streetlights hold halos of swirling snow; rainbows appear if you look at the streetlights and squint. My footsteps the only sound of any human being, I continue the hollow morning walk to school.

Deep breath
Ice in lung
Frog in throat
Lava in belly

Grade eight. Ugh. I have another giant cold sore on my chin. It's ten miles wide and oozing. I do my best to disguise it with my scarf and steel my ego for the taunting that I am about to receive. "Soresees" is the name that gets appointed to the person suffering from a cold sore for the entirety of its duration. This name can also be applied to chickenpox, eczema, bed bug bites, zits, or any other skin ailment. The series of nicknames allotted to the students in our school were never kind, but often so amusing that we were happy to carry the burden when it was our turn. I silently thank the universe that I will never be branded "Nibble-a-cock" like my friend Casper Noviligak because she gave a blowjob to that hotdog on a dare last Thursday.

It took me fifteen minutes to pull these jeans on this morning. They are so tight that it hurts to breathe. Sometimes I have to use a coat hanger to get the zipper up. The tighter the jeans the better, and neon is in; neon leg warmers, neon tights, neon shirts, neon banana clips. We pile our hair as high as it will go, even though the wind destroys our hairdos to the point that every time we come in from outside, the girls' bathroom is a haze of Final Net. We sport Chip and Pepper heat-sensitive colour-changing muscle shirts (leaving us hiding our fluorescent-orange armpits after gym), and pair them with acid-washed jeans and light blue eyeshadow. AC/DC. Dirty deeds and they're done dirt cheap.

The frosted-pink lip gloss clashed with my cold sore so I didn't wear it today. My lips are cracked and chapped and my hair is flying with static electricity and keeps getting into my cold sore. Winter is dry. Like zero humidity. The cold holds moisture hostage. The boys scuff their socks on the carpet and shock the girls with pointed fingers and malicious glee. I hate it.

I want to be the size of an ant, or just disappear. This year everyone got boobs except me. Every morning brings the measuring tape to the mirror in the hopes of the miracle of being suddenly blessed with tits, forever ending the reign of my nickname: Golf Balls. In lieu of breasts, I arrange sheets of toilet paper to make a home nest in my brassiere. The indignities we suffer as children will only grow larger as we get older, so we are told. That seems impossible.

I get good grades in school without putting in much effort. I fail tests on purpose to avoid drawing too much ire from the popular girls, who seemed to think that accomplishing anything scholastically made you vain. School is scary and awkward; I guess it's supposed to be. Sitting still for that long is impossible. My ass is numb. Who made this system? It feels like a slow torture watching the second hand tick by, watching the flakes of dandruff fly around the teacher's head when he stands in the light. How can someone be almost bald and still have dandruff? Getting old is so gross. Watching people slowly rot is unnerving. I listen to the children breathing and sighing. We steal glances at each other. Listening to pencils scratching, we yearn for movement. Listening to the wind howl in screaming freedom, we all feel muted.

Math class. The cute boy peeks up and smiles at me over his math book while holding hands under the table with the pretty girl. I'm aware that he is manipulating me but I still die a little inside. His black hair is in a brush cut and he smells a little mouldy, like his mom took too long to get the clothes into the dryer. He makes up for it with a searing confidence and sharp wit. Brightness. It shocks me every time he looks at me. He has already seen too much in life and his natural propensity for cruelty coupled with the hormones coursing through his body has him playing girls against each other like bristling sled dogs. He still gets to taste them all. I've always hated this social display of jealousy, girls scratching each other's eyes out for boys. If he leaves me alone I can maintain my dignity, but I feel the pull of him in a place that is foreign to me. It is my first real crush. Our teacher is discussing physics.

I think about the equal and opposite reaction to the look the boy just gave me and blush furiously. His girlfriend notices. Shit! I'm in for it after school. Doors open and close, the books in the library call me with their musty elder smell. The clocks rotate. I get my head slammed into my locker at recess, and the school day is over. Thank fuck.

I only work from the waist up

Psychological epidural

Numb

I was entered too young

We were entered too young

Cast in a pit of tar

The more I struggle the deeper I sink

Cold can preserve you Warmth can draw you down

A glance from my daughter Her soft hair tangled and her

giggles echo My blood and brains blasted against the

bathroom wall A text from my mother "I love you"

My body hanging from the stairwell

An accolade, a sweet message,

Stay away from the kitchen knives today

My lover places his hand on the nape of my neck as we kiss

I'm drowned in the bathtub I pity everyone who loves me

because they deserve better A thousand jokes A million lies

as everyone observes someone who walks and talks with leg

and mouth This is the gift rape gives It is not violence against

women It is violence done by men I hang my head And

I stand up tall In the hope we all can heal And I drown

My head full of tar

Butane is my drug of choice these days. It's great to get an actual high instead of the pretend one that we get from rolling up oregano and pretending it's weed. One time we sold a piece of caribou dung to some tourist's kid, telling him it was hashish. When asked if he got high, he replied that it was "really good shit!" We still laugh at that. Butane is clean. I like to steal it from the Co-op store and press the nozzle into my front teeth to release the gas, and inhale it deeply. The stars grow sharper and the colours get brighter. Sound elongates. Everything pixelates, blurs and sharpens simultaneously. Echo becomes my world and the numbness turns into flashes of light while the ground turns into rolling waves. I am a boat. I am a lightning bolt. I belong here in this world where nothing exists. After coming down I will have to hide from my mother for a few hours because she will see the high in my eyes. Her eyes have always known mine. She made them, after all.

———

Country music and loud voices yank me out of sleep. The bedroom door opens a crack. Smoke billows in and the music is louder for an instant while the door is opened, then it softens again once the door is closed. Weight on the bed. I feign sleep and go to the faceless place.

Air becomes thin
flesh could be moved like warm butter
and chewed and swallowed without hurting anyone
where my own insides
can be pulled through my fingers.
Death is uncorrupted.
When you're filthy, you long to be clean.
Where the lights go dim
and reality blurs
and thoughts turn red,
this heartbeat will stop
pumping what others call hopes and dreams
through a cardiovascular nightmare.
Never-ending chambers,
each one darker than the last,
hide everything that is true.
The walls are dancing.
We all have to play the game
and pretend.
I crave rock underfoot
I crave
I crave clear vision
I crave to be
anything but me.
I am thrashing,
gasping for air.

I can't see
Through fog.
I can't feel anything anymore.
Other than the echo in my conscience
that this will pass
One must trust
in a world that has been perfect
in its distribution of chaos.

I am awakened from a deep slumber by the creaking of a
hinge. The door slides open. A column of light enters the
dark room. The music is louder for a moment, a country song.
I can hear a swell of laughter and boisterous merriment in
Inuktitut. The smell of cigarette smoke and booze follows
the sound. An unnamed man enters, a shape, a shadow.

I am sharing a room with an older girl. She came in a
while before; she snores softly on the bed beside mine. I felt
relief when she came to bed, I didn't like being alone in here.
Her teenaged years have not passed her yet. The man creeps
in and sits on her bed. He exhales too sharply when he sits,
an indicator that he has had too much to drink. The smell
of liquor is strong. His breath heavy and thick, he gently
shakes her and asks if she is awake. No answer. I hear shuf-
fling, snapping of elastic, and peeling off of fabric. I chance
a peek: a sliver of sight through an otherwise tightly closed
eye. He has taken her pants off; her pubis is being pinched
between thick fingers. She makes a small sound. He climbs on

top of her and I can see him manoeuvring around. She starts to wake up. I feel a strange sensation in my belly, like I am going down a roller coaster. I hear her murmur, "The little one is on the other bed." He says, "She's just a kid, she's asleep," and continues his endeavour.

It was over soon, squeaking springs and mewling sounds. The feeling in my belly went away and was replaced with disgust. I wasn't brave enough to look again. I just pretended it wasn't happening.

47

Symbol	Sound	Symbol	Sound	Symbol	Sound	Finals	
ᐃ	i	ᐅ	u	ᐊ	a		
ᐱ	pi	ᐳ	pu	ᐸ	pa	ᑉ	p
ᑎ	ti	ᑐ	tu	ᑕ	ta	ᑦ	t
ᑭ	ki	ᑯ	ku	ᑲ	ka	ᒃ	k
ᒋ	gi	ᒍ	gu	ᒐ	ga	ᒡ	g
ᒥ	mi	ᒧ	mu	ᒪ	ma	ᒻ	m
ᓂ	ni	ᓄ	nu	ᓇ	na	ᓐ	n
ᓯ	si	ᓱ	su	ᓴ	sa	ᔅ	s
ᓕ	li	ᓗ	lu	ᓚ	la	ᓪ	l
ᔨ	ji	ᔪ	ju	ᔭ	ja	ᔾ	j
ᕕ	vi	ᕗ	vu	ᕙ	va	ᕝ	v
ᕆ	ri	ᕈ	ru	ᕋ	ra	ᕐ	r
ᕿ	qi	ᖁ	qu	ᖃ	qa	ᖅ	q
ᖏ	ngi	ᖑ	ngu	ᖓ	nga	ᖕ	ng
ᖠ	lhi	ᖢ	lhu	ᖤ	lha	ᖦ	lh

Innuinaktun class. I hate this class. The teacher's dry, brown, papery hands repulse me. His nails have weird white lines underneath them. He is too thin and hunches as if he is about to be kicked. He moves like a nervous rat. He wears yellow-tinted aviator glasses. He smells of victimhood and insecurity. Shaking and desperate, his exhalations sharp and pained as he glances at us. The sides of his mouth are marked with white foam.

His mouth is hungry. His mouth makes sounds that mean Innuinaktun lessons but his eyes are eating us alive. I once saw a picture of him when he was young, being sent off to residential school, dressed in caribou-skin clothing and smiling. He was actually smiling. He didn't have a shroud yet. He is one of those people I can feel. He is what I have already known, and then he does as I have already seen.

The nuance in his hand movements shows us secrets, deep ones that travel underneath the surface of our consciousness. I can tell he was abused by his posture. He usually hunches but becomes taller and throws back his shoulders around subordinates, around victims. He is small. He is defeated. He disgusts me.

I feel deficient in this class. My mother never speaks to me in Inuktitut anymore. Residential schools have beaten the Inuktitut out of this town in the name of progress, in the name of decency. Everyone wanted to move forward. Move forward with God, with money, with white skin and without the shaman's way. It made me wonder what I was not being taught. It made me wonder why the teachings I was receiving felt like sandpaper against my skin. It made me sad to have Inuktitut slip away. It lives under my subconscious just like the secrets of the teacher do.

So much has slipped away these days. The students snicker and gauge each other's interest in the activities given. We cut and paste words from our ancestry onto our paper-doll versions of ourselves and everyone feels a little bit empty.

Shaking while waking. I have gut-wrenching nightmares. They say it's a symptom of a guilty conscience. It's not our fault. We make it our fault. We like to make it huge but Guilt belongs in your back pocket. Guilt and Shame are the ultimate godly gifts. The dreams seem to bubble up from the centre of the earth, consuming my soul and preying on my being. Sometimes the devil comes to impale me, slice me sideways and quarter my loins. These dreams are horrid, but the ones where people get tortured are worse because I can never help them. I'm always being consumed while in the vulnerable state of unconsciousness; a huge weight that is the whole universe comes to rest upon me, to smother me in ineptitude. Making me slow and blind. Impotent. Powerless. Voiceless. Cowardly.

Dreams will follow you into the day to force action, to change what caused the anxiety. We never like to listen to ourselves, even when we know we have to. We plod on ignoring what we must be, what we are meant to be. We are taught to fear our instincts. We must hunt down and fall in love with the Fear, therefore defeating our self-doubt every day. This is followed by joy. This is followed by handing over control. This is followed by lightness. This is followed by freedom. This releases the dreams.

People try to hide from themselves, but I see through people. Everyone can see, for we all have the same instincts that kept previous generations alive. Society dictates the rules of what is acceptable, but in reality there are only the rules of nature. Natural Law. It's impolite to point out a lie. I think it's disrespectful to your own spirit to play into falsehoods. Outward faces and words are usually so different from their true selves and vulnerabilities that people like to hide. I see past them pretending to be who they wish they were. I see them convincing themselves that they are justified in their actions. I see THEM.

The best way to describe the observation is to imagine a face that is made out of Silly Putty that is being animated. The mouth keeps moving with muffled noise but there is a bright light coming out of it and the colour of the light determines what they really feel. Sometimes this light is warming and delicate, and I chase these people around and seek more time with them. There is nothing more beautiful than someone being real.

Sometimes their light is sick and they want to infect you with it, clawing you downwards in a desperate attempt to create safety in numbers. Sometimes the eyes are dead and the light is dead and they are only a body. These are the truly dangerous ones, because there is room for a lost spirit to come and enter their vessel to use it to carry out the spirit's own agenda. Steer clear of these ones. Do not spend too much time around them, because Time is shifting; the trajectory of our meagre existence is mapped out in energetic arteries. The dangerous ones can colour you. They can change your path. Do not eat around them, lest you accidentally consume their energy. Do not touch them; it allows a clearer path for them to enter. Mostly do not try to help them, because it is only like tying rocks to your feet and jumping into the icy waters with them.

I see your face change.

I see you.

ᓯᕗᓕᕕᓂᕗᑦ ᖃᐃᒥᑦᑎ

ᑕᑕᑎᖅᑎᒍᓪᓗ ᓴᙱᓂᕐᒥᒃ

ᕿᓄᐃᓵᕐᓂᕐᒥᒃ

ᓯᕗᓕᕕᓂᕗᑦ ᖃᐃᒥᑦᑎ

ᐃᑲᔪᖅᑎᒍᑦ ᐊᔪᕐᓇᖅᑐᒦᑎᓪᓗᑕ

ᓯᕗᓕᕕᓂᕗᑦ ᖃᐃᒥᑦᑎ

ᓴᐃᒻᒪᖅᑎᑎᒍᑦ ᖃᐅᒪᓂᕐᒧᑦ

ᖁᔭᓐᓇᒦᒃ ᑕᐃᒃᑯᐊ ᓯᕗᓕᕕᓂᕗᑦ

ᖁᔭᓐᓇᒦᒃ ᑕᐃᒃᑯᐊ ᓯᕗᓂᑦᑎᓐᓂ ᐃᓅᓛᖅᑐᑦ

Walking home from school, the country music is loud again. The thumping is metronomic but the screeches and whoops of the listeners are chaotic. The house is shaking with people dancing. High-spirited laughter spills through the glass panes. Going home is never a good idea under these circumstances. The partiers will just demand that I echo their toxicity. Nothing bores me more. They think they are so clever but they are just bleary and repetitive.

I keep walking and continue to the sea ice. My parents' house is only fifty feet away from the immensity of the Arctic Ocean. I alternate taking walks on the water and walks on the land; they feed different parts of my feet and vibrate my femurs at different speeds. The sea seems eternal. She offers comfort in the form of Vast Solidarity. Our Original Home. I wonder if the wind currents could mimic the water currents if they had the same viscosity. The Northern Lights mirror each other on opposite sides of the earth. How much is connected? How much can we see while regulated by blood and flesh? The Ocean Ice can hold so much. Ice prevents decay; it can slow your burden. It can stop it completely by filling your lungs.

Motionless. I am lying on the ice for an unknown amount of time because Time went for a walk. Ice in lung, fear in spleen, and river of blood flowing from my womb. Can the water be cognizant of my own fleshly currents through the ten feet of ocean ice? Can my blood join the ocean currents in ritual? Moon approves. He brings both blood and light upon those long winter nights. Wind on face, rhythm in chaos, and consolation in constellations.

A small sliver of green light begins to pulsate in the sky. Cold bites my face, numbing it after a quick stab of pain. Frostbite. Exhalations are collecting in a thick coating of ice on my scarf but I like it. Northern Lights are always worth the cold. Legend says that if you whistle or scream at them, they will come down and cut off your head. This is ridiculous, but I admit to running home quickly a when the whole horizon is full of light and the movement of the roaring green thunder shakes my vertebrae like dice. Maybe some sound will coax the Northern Lights out of the sky? Sound can only help beckon them.

Arqsarniq. I sing for you. Humming shakily at first, thin tendrils of sound. The trepidation dissolves and a throbbing vibratory expulsion of sound emerges. Thicker, richer, heavier. Sound is its own currency. Sound is a conduit to a realm we cannot totally comprehend. The power of sound conducts our thoughts into emotions that then manifest in action.

Sound can heal.

Sound can kill.

Sound is malleable. Sound can be a spear or a needle. Sound can create the wound and then stitch it. Sound can cauterize and materialize. No one can hear my song but the Northern Lights.

My body grows warmer and I can feel columns of clarity being paved from core to skin. The swirling columns leave my body and grow high into the sky and deep into the water. I am a pillar, gorging on the dimensions we sense but never see. The Northern Lights grow larger, a sliver morphing into a great curtain of movement that pulsates from east to west, parallel to my form on the ice. The lights become bolder and grow closer. They seem curious, drawn by the sound of flesh and my meagre offering of spirit. My ears plug and pop with pressure and the warmth in my core starts to turn into heat. The lights begin to blur and I swear they are calling me backwards/forwards in Time, back to a time before I was born and where I will return to after I die.

The lights join my song with a sound of their own: a high-pitched ringing mixed with the crackling snap of electricity. I can feel it on my skin and in my belly. A dog howls, and I can also hear someone weeping in agony a long ways away, but a long time ago.

The Northern Lights grow larger still and begin to morph into faces, blurry, omnipotent, healing and death-dealing. They sharpen and I see Aunties and Great-grandmothers. I see Ancestors and future children; the young ones are just developing and preparing their spirits for the next rotation of Earth Journey. It takes millennia to return to Earth after we die. I weep at the majesty of our ancestors, and give thanks to the opportunity to witness them. Tears freeze. The heat in my core starts to burn and the world turns upside down.

Then there is silence. Emptiness. Only the wind is taking up space. I open my eyes and awaken from what must have been a dangerous dream. My chest and throat hurt. I had unzipped my coat, seemingly in offering. The cold had its way with me. Ice in lung, Ice on chest, Ice in heart. Zipping back up and running home to the now comforting thumping of Johnny Cash's bass.

Ananaa asks me where I have been. "Out walking," I say and retreat to the bathroom, where I blow my nose and flush out the bright and glowing green substance that the Northern Lights have left in my head. It is squirming like larvae.

This tapestry has not been woven

By accident

Silken deception

Falsehoods twisted into each fibre

The blue water lost to a sea of red

Red tide

Poisonous intent disguised by the shine

Of the thread

When *we* weave,

We weave past longing, past glory, past greed

Weave the hunger

Weave the need

To conquer to vanquish to quell

With quill with seed

We plant ideas

With bullets we heed

We raise fists we draw

Fine lines to hold each other

Up against the ships

Sails canvas story silk

Survival is the only guide

We weave our own sinew

Make a net

To catch those not yet dead,

Those drowning on dry land.

We will harvest the truth.

We will collect the rent.

This tapestry is being rewoven.

There are too many foxes this year. It usually happens in a four- to seven-year cycle, all dictated by the rains and melt. Plenty of rain means that the lemmings and their young are forced above ground, where they are easy prey for the fox pups. If too many foxes survive, there won't be enough food for them when winter comes along.

They populate the dump, and all garbage cans in town are full of them. I once saw five foxes in one rusted garbage can. Some become rabid and all the children need to walk to school carrying a stick, preferably with a nail in it. All of the houses in Nunavut must be built on stilts because the permafrost makes it impossible to sink foundations. The space under the house makes a perfect hiding place for foxes. Foxes are such steadfast and mysterious creatures. If a wolf and a lynx mated, perhaps their love child would be Fox, who seems to embody the uncanny agility and size of a cat coupled with the strength and durability of a canine. My friend Eugene had to get rabies shots in his tummy after being bitten; it did not look pleasant. I was proud of him for not crying. Let's avoid rabies.

My father and I go out with the handgun to kill some foxes. Satisfying dry cracks and snaps of sound as the gun goes off. I feel like a hero for an instant, saving the foxes from a slow death of starvation. My father is strong, self-assured. I hope that someday this fortitude emerges from my fragile psyche. The foxes run. The foxes die. I mourn them, but I understand that there is danger in mourning for those who would not mourn for you in return. Empathy is for those who can afford it. Empathy is for the privileged.

Empathy is not for Nature.

Our family had dogs that would have to be buried or put out of their misery. My father always took care of his work, even if it was mercy-killing our family pets. He did it without allowing room for regret. He just did it. Like how we are all born, like how we all die. No choice, only action. These foxes will die of starvation; better to put them out of their misery. These foxes will harm schoolchildren; better to put them out of their misery. These humans will destroy the earth; better to put them out of their misery. Right now we are Earth Eaters, but I want to be a blood lover, an oil spewer, someone with a great wingspan, a spirit sipper, a flesh licker. I want it all. I kill a mountain of foxes in my dreams. Mercy killings, but I do enjoy it.

Speaking of tonight's dream: The sky is the kind of orange that only happens in the fall after the midnight sun begins to retreat. Rolling hills of sandstone rock look like pages of books, making it impossible to walk except for thin paths of spines or else you lose your balance. The path is guarded by sentries, hundred-foot-tall polar bears, who are all facing south. I must pass them one by one. I'm terrified but know it must be done. These are beasts of Protection and Warning. I am thankful they remain still as I meekly seek passage through their domain. The sun is setting and the sky is criss-crossed with airplanes, each leaving plumes of thick grey sickness. None of the planes can fly past the line of sentries. One half of the sky lives while the other half dies. Dead skies. The sentries can only hold the balance for so long.

We ARE the land, same molecules, and same atoms. The land is our salvation. Save Our Souls.

The land is our salvation. Breathe. Fuck. Feel.

Empathy is for those who can afford it.

Ice will crack, blood will flow. Sun in Ice. Ice in lung.

Speaker of tongues.

There are so many ways to be empty.

Ice in lung, flush of cheek, blood in mouth.

There is a storm of light, of gravity, of silence. No ground nor sky. I wander through the electricity and the void. Something is very wrong. Something is magnetic. It is calling me from a mile away. I listen to the calling. It gets louder and all of a sudden out of the sound, you are there. You are at my feet, but you lie on nothing. I turn my head towards you slowly. You are grey. Every inch of you is a mottled, sickly grey. A dead colour. Iridescent streaks of silver begin swirling under your skin. Small whirlpools of activity. Life? I realize that the movement comes from blistering and searing. It's as if you are being burned with a blowtorch in a hundred places, and the whorl of colour is the only evidence of your suffering. The boiling and burning hypnotize me. This is almost beautiful, until you look at me.

Our eyes meet. Black eye on black eye. The panic is a gift from yours to mine. The agony and the fear lock us together in a holy union. Your mouth opens and emits a toothless scream. Your hair falls out. The torture. The Pain. Your mouth opens wider and wider until the skin begins to rip. When we skin a caribou, we often separate the skin from the flesh by inserting our hands between the membranes and then peeling. This is happening to you with invisible hands, and then the skin reattaches itself so you can feel that same thing again and again. Oil begins to seep from all of your orifices. Death is a thousand times more desirable than this. You lie at my feet. Writhing. Undying. Pleading. I am frozen. There is nothing I can do but look into your seyes and bear witness. I will always bear witness.

Where have I fallen?

We rolled the dice and

You got a six and

I got a one

And now the Deep Knowing is gone.

Now the tears belong to others,

And all we can do is yearn.

There is a limb of mine

That still belongs to you

It hurts like any ghost limb would

Leave me to the memories

Of your braid,

Leave me with my hollow decisions

And foolish ways.

Because I still pine

I still pine.

The river was frozen. It paved a long, undulating path, smooth and white. The snow was blinding because the sun had come back to bounce off it. It is an ocean of white that covers every surface. From the skies fall the light, minuscule flakes that get blown around easily. The kind of flakes that love to kiss sundogs and leave a thin film of moisture on your face. The flakes of snow that blow up your sleeves and try to get to your heart. The kind of snow that still buries our dead. I drove my snowmobile under the river bridge, the windshield almost scraping the bottom of the steel girders. Continuing on my frosty way to Mount Pelly, I rode my snowmobile fast and absorbed the bumps with my strong thighs. I was elastic. I was powerful, the speed creating calmness. The day was crisp and the wind penetrating. It was one of those days when it seems as if you can see farther than other days. Eagle eyes. The landscape reflected all the morphing memories of every northern place I had been. The snow fought back, my machine riding waves of movement. Whiteness forever.

I noticed something strange in the distance. There seemed to be a two-storey house at the base of Mount Pelly, a mansion by Cambridge Bay standards. A Nunavut HAP house mansion. It was absolutely unheard of to have a house like that there, and I began to suspect that this was a dream. The house approached much too quickly and offered a serene welcome. I walked into the house and looked around. The bright sun made the day wholesome. In the kitchen my brother was chopping tuktu for some stir-fry but he had a massive raven head. He looked at me and squawked in raven language and I understood him perfectly. He said, "Hey, Sis, check this shit out! HAHAHAHAA! I love being a fucking raven! SQUAWK!" We were laughing our heads and beaks off and I heard an indescribable sound downstairs. It sounded like a glow.

I followed the sound. The pine stairwell was a very long and steep so the descent took an incalculable amount of time. I arrived at a wood-panelled porch with two giant picture windows. The sun was so bright that everything was sparkling outside, and there was a slight howl to the wind. Rows of miniature crystal animals were lined up on the windowsills, shining. Raven. Tulugak. Caribou. Tuktu. Polar Bear. Nanuk. Lemming. Avingnak. Wolf. Amarok. Movements that were barely perceptible were teasing me from inside the figures. Were they calling me? I shrugged it off, attributing it to the glare of the springtime sun.

The windows took up two full walls of the porch, and that's when I truly knew it was a dream because a porch like that would cost a fortune to heat. I was admiring the landscape in complete stillness when a small shadow appeared in the distance. It moved sideways and slowly began to approach the house. I squinted my eyes but could not make out the form, which seemed to change its gait every few metres. Long and darting, sinuous. It was a fox! As he came closer I realized that he was huge, man sized. My fear was overridden by his maleness, by his grace. I could see every hair on him, white and perfect. The wind blew around him and his black eyes spoke to me, "Let me in."

The pitch in his mind-voice opened a vault of understanding in me. This was not the first time this fox had come to me, and it wouldn't be the last. His voice was the light; his voice was all the darkness. It was the deepest, smoothest voice I had ever heard. My flesh was softened, my will blinded. The world opened beneath me, and the dawning of what life really meant was projected through him. He shot me with truth and the burden of our bodies. I saw in an instant the spiritual world we all ignore. Like the radio waves we can't see, it is everywhere. Our bodies trapped in our dark masses, we have forgotten how to see. I saw the parliament of the spirit law and the congregation that forced us into flesh. When they spoke and I saw a chain, a spiral of generations, and a curse laid two hundred years ago upon the fox clan.

Fox had gotten greedy and ate all the lemmings one year, therefore the raven queen died. She cursed Fox as her last breath left her, casting a screaming inkblot on the future well-being of all foxes. The Fox clan had been weakened since.

I opened the door, and he brushed past me on all fours. His scent hit me, so pungent that it almost stung my nose. It also opened a pathway of urgency within me. I was deeply agitated, but everything seemed to be moving in slow motion. His scent penetrated me, travelling down my esophagus and leaving warmth in my throat and paving a highway into my belly. My bones seemed to loosen. I couldn't move.

Then he spiralled his limber body onto a chair, sitting like a man. He had a huge black and orange cock, veiny and pulsating. I knew I had to put him in my mouth. I was feeling a mixture of revulsion and an uncontrollable tingle in my mouth, almost an itch. His cock would satisfy it.

I put him in my mouth and started to suck on him. Smooth and delicious, there was no room for words. His urgency accumulated throughout his torso, his legs, every-thing was coming towards me. All of him collecting like a bullet. He got so hard in my mouth that it was like sucking on a stone, and I couldn't budge him even a millimetre. He exploded but I knew not to let it down my throat. I felt a release in me too, and felt a gushing hot liquid between my legs. I looked down and there was a glowing golden puddle between my knees. His cum was silver and my whole throat

was emitting a bright yellow light, so bright that you could see into my head. I knew if I swallowed his cum, it would change the lifeline of my clan for generations, we would have the fox way in our movements, and part of the curse would be carried as well.

I walked over to the door and opened it, and let his cum out of my mouth. It tasted so good it was a hard thing to do. As it landed it melted the snow and grew giant lichens and flowers for a fifty-foot radius. I turned back to him and the whole inside of my mouth and throat felt so good I could hardly see. Blinded and dazed, I wanted to live in that sublime moment always. It's the best I have ever felt. He gave me a fox figure to place alongside the others and I understood. I had cleansed him of Raven's curse.

So limber, my fox. He got off the chair and gracefully left. He looked back just once, and I saw myself through his eyes. I was his saviour and was covered in light, almost weightless, like a jellyfish in a giant fishbowl. Knowing, lonely, perfect. No other king or queen could come to me for cleansing for another few hundred years, and my offspring would all carry an instinct in them. The knowing. The healing. The Cleansing.

Remember that time when the sun

Sat sideways just to please you?

Orange sun-faced and long-shadowed,

We shunned the rest of the world and rested cross-legged

Only to uncross them and run

We cracked open pops and unzipped our souls

To encapsulate the wind and

Placate the restlessness

We didn't know we would spend the rest of our lives running

Or we would have slowed down

Remember that time the river ran backwards

Just to please you?

The eddies grabbed our toes and travelled up our legs

The sun much sharper it reminded us

That those eddies wanted to eat us

Numb and bloodless

Toes curdled we

Ran until the river forgot we were there

Remember the time the wind stopped breathing

Just to please you?

White-cheeked frostbite with alternating hands

To cover the pain

Backs to the wind for protection

We did not need vision

Only the moon was guiding our laughter

When you fell and all stood still
The world stopped spinning and I realized
Your eyes were the centre of the earth

Another morning, another warning. Time to numb out in
school again. Today in health class we are taking sex ed. It's
so embarrassing. As if any of these boys know what a clitoris
is. Our teacher has massive breasts and wears low-cut shirts.
That's all the sex ed anyone is getting: have big tits and
show them off and get all the attention. The boys make
excuses to ask her for help as I retire to the lowest rung
of the feminine hierarchy.

Off-colour jokes and overcompensation do not mask my
lack of actual tits. I get ignored. At least I am menstruating;
that means it is only a matter of time. The cute boy laughs
at one of my Pee-wee Herman impersonations, resulting in
a withering glare from pretty girl. Lately the glances from
him have become more frequent. Noticing him notice me ani-
mates me with pride. I can draw giggles from him. Laughter
IS the best medicine. Even for humiliation. He shares a smoke
with me at recess and I go home feeling like Jessica Rabbit.
Our family is having ground caribou shepherd's pie for dinner.

There is no loud music or unexpected visitors today. There are many thanks to be given.

The sun slowly returns. Lunch Time Sunshine! Nothing feels better than the return of the sun. The sun peeks over the horizon and tells you to endure. "I am coming to save you from yourselves," says the Sun. "I am coming to save you from Moon, who has bullied you into submission and stolen your will to survive." Moon uses the violence of the cold. Sun grows more powerful to shoo away the freeze. Sun grows strong as Earth turns to face her. She gives you life, and hope. North is in love with Sun. North is in love with the Life she brings. Open your legs and she will give you a birth. Open your mouth and she will pour flowing light down your throat. The famine will subside. She grabs her drums and sings.

Ice will crack
Blood will flow
Sun in Ice
Ice in lung
Eater of tongue
Speaker of tongue
Speaking in tongues

My mother is a quiet woman, a stoic woman. My mother is a strong woman. She grew up on the land. Sod houses in the summer and igloos in the winter. I can only imagine the power that was blown around the land by the massive wind, unhindered by Christianity. What logic was maintained while at the mercy of such elements? There is no logic when molecules slow from the cold. What governs the Force of the cold? Sometimes I can feel a tickle at the very base of my coccyx: the Old Knowing. My mother was a child of transition; government relocation, the shift into capitalism, and the moulting of the Shaman Skin led to the generation of Christian Rules, Blind Faith, and Shame. Christians seem to love Shame: shame on your body, your soul, your actions and inactions. Put a cork in all of your holes and choke on the light of God. We have no power over a universe that we can barely comprehend. We are truly armed with nothing. Our ideologies impoverish us. They give us a reason to destroy Earth and ourselves along with it. How can Christians shame the process of welcoming spirit into flesh? How can Christians say we are born in sin?

The Earth calls us back into her
Just as the Earth is being pulled
Back into her origin
The one giant breath
The universe exhaled
All of us out
Therefore the universe
Will inhale
All back in again
Upon our deaths
The Earth welcomes us into
her bosom
Turns us into plants and oil and wind
Churns us into more life

I would call my parents and say I was sleeping over at your house. You would call your parents and say you were sleeping over at my house.

I don't know how we fit so many children in the old nursing station porch. There was nowhere else to go for shelter, because we had all told our parents that we were at each other's houses. There was no other shelter from the screaming winds. We shivered, nervously laughing in our tight denim and big hair so meticulously sprayed into blooming fountains. The snow had blown into our hair, and now it was melting. Our magnificent towers were becoming flaccid mockeries of themselves. Our mascara ran down our faces, beauty problems at minus forty.

The porch was about ten feet by ten. There were seven kids in it. We lit up all the butts we had picked off the ground. I had a big cold sore on my chin. I thought I could distract from it by putting on a lot of shimmery blue eyeshadow. I don't think it worked very well. Our breath slowly stopped showing as our body heat warmed up the small room. What should we do in this little porch? Someone touched my ass. I slapped his grubby little hand away. Let's play a dare game!

We simply went around in a circle, taking turns, collectively agreeing on a dare for whoever's turn it was. If you failed to do your dare, you were banished from the shelter. This system immediately went awry when a girl started to cry because she had to kiss the ugly boy. Fuck this. We left the shelter and went our separate ways.

Your uncle was out partying. We crashed at his place. After raiding the fridge we put a movie on, I think it was *The Dark Crystal*.

We were coaxed out of our slumber by a thick smacking sound. You uncle was a gentle man, slight and benign. He had been dating a very aggressive woman. I never understood how he put up with the abuse. We heard a woman weeping softly through the walls. We could hear him quietly asking her, "There, are you happy now?" and another thick, wet thud would come. Tears, snot, blood. Wet noises. She just took it. There was no struggle. I knew what a fight sounds like. This was quieter, more intimate.

I understood. She hated herself so much that she would berate him and beat him over and over until she got what she wanted, the proof that she deserved to be beaten. Their love for each other was indistinguishable from the hate they felt for themselves. Sometimes children see more clearly than adults. They loved the cycle of self-hatred and forgiveness. They perpetuated a perfect, violent machine. "You must like it." Smack. "You make me do this." Smack.

We plug our ears. Fall back asleep, not daring to move lest we alert them to our presence. "Let's go," you whisper, nudging me. It's quiet in the house now. We tiptoe out of the bedroom. The sun is up. I adjust my eyes, looking for my jean jacket. I can smell the blood. There are pools of it on the floor. The cat had tracked it all over the living room. There are red paw prints everywhere.

I peek in the room. The couple is sleeping together, embracing. Forgiven. Bruised. Bloodied.

We walk home. We part ways at the stop sign. We never speak of this night again.

Competition ignites itself
Like that time the glint off the midnight sun
turned the razor blade blind
for a moment and I accidentally sliced
You way too deep
Who can handle the biggest wound?
Who does not yield to pain or blood?
Poker face birth face rape face

Pain is not forever
But it is the doorway into the next realm
So we practise pain

When there is none around
We create it and rehearse it
Hoping to prove our strength
Hoping to distract from fear
Hoping to survive
Survival is competition and also ignites itself
Like that time you just had to go
To get the box of salt to rub in
To all of our wounds
Screaming, crying, laughing
None of us were strong enough
None of us could hang on
To the straight face, the toughness
We are children
Needing nurture not razor blades

1982

I was seventeen. Sent back home from residential school after
a suicide attempt. Not a bad place all in all, Cambridge Bay.
Curfews and duties seemed confining but comforting after
the chaos of high school. The wind blew high and we were
freezing. My friend and I were hot for a party and dressed for
it, though the temperature dipped down past minus forty.
Seventeen is an age of freedom.

"There's a party at my aunt's house," she said. We weighed
the pros and cons. Her aunt was not one to be fucked with.
When she was drinking she was volatile. She was the self-
appointed party police. But the buzz would make it worth
our while if we could finagle a few beers to start the hunt off.

We walk in, the all-too-familiar smell of the clan, the
blaring country music. The cigarette smoke saturates my
clothing on impact. Ashtrays scattered around the room.
Conflict lurking under smiles, waiting to pounce after a
few more drinks. Silent Sam is lurking.

My glasses fog up. I am almost blind without them. I feel

a presence before I feel his touch. A hand slides up my leg. I can hardly feel it because the cold has almost frozen me through the tight denim, a shaky and thin hand, and a familiar hand. I know who it is before I can see him. His touch is like a bony finger that penetrates me and fuses with the bones in my spine. For years, this man would touch me during his class. Under tables, sneaking his hand in my pants. Touching my little-girl parts. After a while I got used to it, even felt envious when he touched other kids.

I smile down at him. Ask him if he would like to join me for a smoke outside. I'm not six years old anymore. I get him outside. He's pretty drunk and I smile as I hit him as hard as I can. He starts to lose his balance and I nudge him the rest of the way as he tumbles down the stairs. They are metal stairs, serrated to prevent slippage. I watch in glee as he lands at the bottom. He is drunk enough that he's flaccid, and doesn't break anything.

"Someone fell down the stairs!" I exclaim to the party. My friend puts her boots on to investigate. People pile out the door to see what happened. He is unconscious but breathing as he is dragged up the stairs and back into the party. My friend's aunt starts yelling about how he must have been pushed. We take turns yelling back and forth, and the huge woman nearly lifts me off the ground by my lapels before we escape, tears, laughter, and adrenaline coursing through the night. We are free.

Sedna the Sea Goddess came before Christianity. She
came from the time when the land was our Lord, and
we were her servants. Sedna had lost her mother at a young
age, and approached puberty without the comfort and
guidance that can only come from a mother. She and her
father lived alone on a small island. Tormented by their
grief for years, they finally settled into a happy existence.
They grew lonely for more family and Atata longed for
grandchildren. Sedna was nearing the time of Blooming.
She could hunt as well as she could sew, and often left with
her dog team for days at a time. She was capable and strong,
intelligent and beautiful.

Once Sedna came of age her father ventured out in the
kayak to find her a worthy husband. He wanted to respect his
long-deceased wife by naming a child after her. Like a stitch
that is continued, a naming could bring back the quirks
and knowledge of the deceased. One can love the deceased
through the namesake.

Father came back with many suitors, for Sedna was coveted for her endowments. She sternly rejected every single one, insisting she was not ready to be married. Though her father was disappointed, he relented. "She will want to marry in the future," he thought.

This idea was thwarted the day she tearfully approached him and confessed that she was pregnant. Blind rage overtook him and he asked who the father was. It seems there was a shapeshifter among them. Sedna's loneliness and longing had called forth the shapeshifter in her lead dog. They spent weeks at a time hunting and fornicating together as he transformed into a human. He would return to dog form when they got home. She confessed to consummating with him even while he was in canine form.

Her father decided this was punishable by death and grabbed her thick braids and tossed her over his kayak. He paddled out to sea as quickly as possible and threw her into the freezing water. "Atata, NO!" she begged as she clutched on to the side of the kayak, almost capsizing it.

He brought out his hunting knife and chopped off her fingers. He wanted nothing more than to serve her death. Sedna sank. The blood her fingers released clotted and formed into ocean beings, and they were her pets. They allowed her to breathe and live under the water. She became the master of all sea creatures. Her love for her pets grew as strong as her distain for Humanity.

Sedna began to enjoy keeping all the sea creatures away from the humans by tucking them into her now miles-long hair. She liked to watch the humans starve. The only way to placate her was to send a shaman down to the bottom of the ocean to sing her lullabies and comb her hair in the hopes that she would release some of the creatures for human consumption and alleviate the famine.

Wait. I need to talk to Sedna and tell her to keep her treasures. Humans have damned themselves and it has nothing to do with Satan, it has only to do with greed. What will Sedna do when she hears the seismic testing?

Another day, another dollar. I even have a job stocking shelves at the Northern Store now. The clicking of the tills and the pricing gun makes me think of insect colonies desperately constructing a Trojan Caribou to sneak me out of the store. I smell a thousand hands, toss a thousand sighs into empty boxes for disposal. Wipe off dusty fingerprints from expired cans of whole chickens. We sold out of Klik. Move the older produce up to the front so people hastily grab them first. We listen to the couples argue over what to have for dinner. We listen to the parents say no and the parents say yes to children. We smoke in the back room and go through litres of drip coffee. The apron keeps slipping off my waist.

A black eye on Saturday. Maybe six. Maybe she deserved it. Turn your head the other way if the shoplifter is too thin. Many hugs. Heartfelt greetings. Whispered secrets. We are the walls. We shuffle down the aisles and take stock of the community.

We congregate. I make out with the butcher in the freezer during breaks. I'm growing breasts and I'm proud of them. The town is small but it is warm. Everyone knows one another. Death and Life walk together. Someone is found frozen by Cape Cockburn. Someone committed suicide. Someone is pregnant. Merry Christmas. Happy Halloween. Stock the seasons watch the deaths. See the new babies. Stock the formula. The vanilla and Listerine have to be sold from behind the till because kids buy it and drink it. I steal a *Playboy* magazine and feel inadequate, then give it to Best Boy in offering. I lie awake at night thinking about the butcher and his boner.

Walking to school on a Thursday, and a fox is staring at me. He is under the hamlet-office stairs. We are alone. It is the Morning Darkness. He holds my gaze for too long. Brazen, fearless. The snow is the dry crystalline kind, like small diamonds everywhere that are easily blown around. Not the hard crust and crunch snow but the kind that absorbs sound rather than making it. Eddies of snowflakes swirl around my legs. What would happen if I did what Fox's eyes beckon me to do?

I take a step towards him. After gathering all of my Peace into a small ball inside my chest, I send it to him. His shoulders relax and he comes out from under the steps. My fingertips and lower back feel strange, they are throbbing and uncomfortable. I'm tingling all over. Some children yell from not too far away and Fox spooks. Darn it. Next time I'll see what he wants. Curiosity killed the fox.

In love with ripe gaze

I show you my teeth

Through a mouth barely open

Glint tooth

Wet tooth

Shy tooth

Engorged by vast grips

I show you my teeth

Through a mouth mostly open

Molars lost in whimpers

Tongue smooth

Sharp tooth

Giant tooth

Numbed by lost fists

I show you my teeth

Picked up off the floor

Split tooth

Growl tooth

Dead tooth

The storm has caused a whiteout. Thick flakes of snow coupling with ferocious wind. The snowflakes turn tiny and reveal seven sundogs on the horizon. The light is blazing. It's the New Sun. The flakes turn fat again and take the visions away. The snow begins to oscillate between thick and thin flakes in a breath like rhythm, causing chaos. I am a witness. I am naked but not cold. We are in spirit flesh form. We walk towards the sun. Wandering on the land, I slice some meat off my own bones to eat. It is the only flesh available and my spirit is starving. It doesn't hurt. I am hungry, hungry for justice, hungry for truth. My flesh keeps growing back but the scars are bad. The scars are too tough to eat so I keep cutting off pieces in new zones of fresh flesh. We reach bone on both calves. My spine is elastic. I am grey and numb, hungry. It's getting colder. I feel nothing.

The wind picks me up off my feet and places me near the shore. The wind wants to help feed my belly. What great fortune that Wind is in a good mood, for she can kill on a whim. The ocean is inexplicably open. There is never open water this time of year. I need to feed. We find some arctic tern eggs near the shore and suck them up; life sprouts new hope in my core. Golden fluid, so hot, travels and shines out of my throat like the sun.

The sun talks to my throat in recognition. I strengthen. I grow, spine straightening and gold spreading. My arms turn into tentacles and I whip the water, pulling eggs out of arctic chars' bellies with an alarming precision. The gold spreads to my eyes and down my fingers. My spine clicks together like Lego pieces and we grow ten feet. I am deadly. I am ravenous. The fish eggs tickle my throat and make my eyes slant and ears twitch. More gold. The horizon presents an electrical storm. Grey black blue rushing towards us. The sun grows afraid and throws some stars into the sky to distract the storm. The electricity absorbs the stars and grows stronger. The sun surrenders, taking her dogs with her into the ocean. I must leave. The only vessel available is a large ice floe. The wind shifts, and I am being swept out to sea.

Cast adrift, I am fat and windburnt. Then comes fear. The floe starts to break up. The ocean is eating the ice, licking and chewing on it. Large cracks form in the floe and the water is calling my name. I will die in the frozen ocean. Humans cannot survive in the frigid water, even in spirit form (most times). The ice breaks into small pieces and I am plunged into the water. It is so cold that it burns. Treading water and feeling the life leave my body, I accept.

I succumb. The pieces of ice have quadrupled in number and have become too small to grasp. These small pieces morph into miniature polar bears, dozens of them. They make mewling noises while they swim alongside my flank. It's an indecipherable language but I am aware they are attempting to comfort me. One bear grows large and swims beside me, his sphere of reality warming the ocean for me. He has given me his corporality. The ocean is like a warm bath.

I mount his back and ride him. My thighs squeeze him and pulse with a tingling light. We are lovers. We are married. He swims with incredible strength and we travel quickly. He keeps me safe and I am drunk on his dignity. The smaller bears shrink, only to be eaten by engorged shrimp. The ocean grows hot with life after the offering of food. My skin melts where there is contact with my lover. The ocean and our love fuse the polar bear and me. He is I, his skin is my skin. Our flesh grows together. His face is my pussy and she is hungry. My legs sprout white fur that spreads all over me. I can feel every hair form inside of me and poke through tough bear-skin. My whole body absorbs him and we become a new being. I am invincible. Bear mother, rabbit daughter, seal eater. Bear lover, human lover, ice pleaser. I will live another year.

Tastes like an echo

When I saw you haloed by the Arctic moon

Sundogs around your head

The moon slicing

Bitter darkness

We sipped the air

It was too cold to chug

Alcohol was our excuse

To steal a snowmobile

And ride away from life

To the far cabin

So we may chart our bodies

And share flesh

We rode so free

Until we ran out of fuel

And you ran all the way

Back to town

I timed my exhalations

As the cold knocked on my lungs

And slapped my cheeks

The Moon awoke

He became brighter than the sun

And told me to have your child

He told me

Then you emerged out of the twenty-four-hour darkness

The gas can strapped to your head

Inuk style

And I died with longing

As the calm drowned me

Science class. The chubby boy beside me is wearing tight yellow track pants that are pulled up too high on his waist. I can see his cock and balls. It makes me uncomfortable but also fills me with a strange glee. He has not showered in a while and has very greasy hair. I draw a picture of him and send it to my best friend across the room via paper airplane. My friend and I are separated in every class because we cannot keep a straight face and stay quiet. She's like a battery pack for my rebel machine.

I feel remorseful picking on Yellow Pants but it seems that in order to maintain any standing in this hierarchical house of horrors you must get close to the Alpha by shitting on Beta. The Alpha is pretty and malicious; she dictates the social environment with an iron fist. All the girls flock around her trying to gain favour in the hope she won't become displeased and sic the rest of the pack onto her. I skulk around her periphery, hoping to skirt the fine line between being cool enough to not get my ass kicked and

geeky enough to be ignored. It works most days. The boys
covet her attention as well. She dates the best boy, the cute
one. He is agile and intelligent, belligerent and cocksure.
He is brown and dreamy. I usually cannot even look at him,
but today he came up to Yellow Pants and me and asked if
we wanted to come to his friend's house after school. I turned
red and said yes. Alpha is laughing at me. Yellow Pants gives
me a dirty look. He wants Best Boy for himself.

After the bell rings we follow him down the street. It's
storming and visibility is low. We show up at a delapidated
matchbox house. It is already dark again. It is the After
School Dark. The rusted hinges complain when the door
is opened. There are holes punched into the plywood panelling. Walls come in all forms. Let's punch holes in them.
Some of the doors have been ripped off their hinges. The
furniture is threadbare and the cupboards hardly have any
food. Three of us have shown up, and we join the two boys
that live here. I have no idea where their parents are. The
boys are eating pilot biscuits and lard and I am aware this
is their dinner. "Always be thankful for all that you have,"
my mother told me. There was plenty of famine in the past,
in our history. Famine can live in your bones and be passed
on to future generations just like your hair colour. There
are many ways to be empty. Let's fill all the holes and punch
all the walls. We get some plastic bags and go into the
back room.

There are rusty metal-framed bunk beds on one side of the room and a single foam mattress on the floor. There are no sheets on the stained foam mattress but a threadbare blanket clings to one corner of it. The windows have garbage bags tacked over them for curtains and we lock the door by jamming a butter knife into the door frame. We stuff some socks into the hole where the doorknob used to be. We have some naphtha, gas, nail polish, rubber cement, and Wite-Out. It's a Bring Your Own Solvents party and I want to let the colours shine. We take turns sharing the bags, not caring if we drool into them. My favourite is the rubber cement and it makes me sad when I have to give it away. Then I stop caring which one I have and there is only the High. Only fragmented faces and the sounds are filtered through a black hole. Bright flashes of colour are changing and dancing to the cadence of my breath. In a moment of spontaneity I walk over to Best Boy and kiss him. He kisses back. His flesh simply becomes heat and his teeth grow into mine until it starts to hurt so we stop. Our mouths are bleeding. We begin to laugh so hard we are crying. He walks me home. Ice in lung, flush of cheek, and solvents in heat.

THAT TIME

Your skinny legs and bucked teeth
Gave no hint of your scathing bravado
Even the Big Girls were afraid of you,
steering clear
of your sudden slaps and rigid kicks
I watched you pull on two pairs of pants
to hide your frail toothpick legs
while you told me you'd kick me in the cunt
if I ever fucked with you
You told me your mom told you
to stand up for yourself
no matter what
Even though you only reached our chins
you stood up for me too
That Time
in the Summer Midnight I wanted to be brave
like you
So we stole my parents' quad
and opened the gas tank to breathe in
The excitement
The iridescence
The speed
We crashed into the church

after getting drunk on the wind

As you lay motionless I found out what prayer was

begging that you breathe again

That Time

we lost our hash in the musk-ox rug

and laughed until we were crying

Biting into orange rinds just because

the citrus blew our minds

That Time

We shared men without jealousy

and shared our love secretly

Then my time came to protect you

the night he wanted you but

you didn't want him back

I threw him down the stairs

and I finally felt strong enough for you

That Time we made love

after you grew up so beautifully

Our Secret Summer

I visited you once in adulthood

you had moved South

Where the trees

breathe in salt water

I watched your children breathing in

salt water too

The Ocean dancing in their eyes
instead of Ice
Then you died inexplicably
Buck-toothed girl
I hope you reached peace

It's just the morning and it's already a Bad Day. Alpha found out about the kiss. I'm going to get my ass kicked after school for sure. Moping about it won't help. The gym teacher's breath smells like actual shit and he's chosen today to have the longest and most uplifting, morale-boosting, intimate talk at me while I cringe in the corner. How can he not know that poop is coming out of his face? Can't he smell it? I ask to sit out today's class but he keeps going on and on about never giving up. I'm too embarrassed to tell him that I have my period. "Moral tenacity develops into technical fortitude" is his motto. We play volleyball in gym class. We lose because I suck at it. The deep-red-faced embarrassment of letting my whole team down because I'm too afraid to be good at the Thing is stoking the flames of insecurity.

I strategically act up in class to try and win a detention. It's cowardly but it works most days, since Alpha won't care to stick around to kick my ass if I have a half-hour detention. I've never been ashamed of being a coward. I prefer the term ultra-cautious. The bell rings. One hundred lines of "I will not tickle the teacher" and off I skulk, making arbitrary small talk with the janitor to extend the time in the safety of the school. I exit from the back door and scurry underneath the building. There are large rips in the metal meshing so this timeworn route can be used for escape. I hear footsteps approaching from around the corner. Time to be silent. If Anana had made my parka cover white, I would be camouflaged in the snow. I wish to employ the remarkable tactic that many Arctic animals do, shedding coats and changing colours with the seasons. Camouflage equals survival. Snow White and Brown Betty.

I wait to make sure the footsteps are receding. Sensing movement, I realize there is someone down here with me. It's Fox. He's looking at me again. I have to decide whom to be more afraid of, rabies or Alpha and company. Alpha wins the Fear Game and Fox is slowly making his way to me, scurrying left, then scurrying right. Remaining still with intent, then circling. Finally Fox becomes comfortable and is a mere foot away from me, face to face. He smells a lot better than the gym teacher. There is a rising heat in my belly as he looks at me.

Fox is more beautiful than any human I've ever seen. I can feel him. Clean, strong, devoted to survival, and unburdened by all the falsehoods that humans subconsciously subscribe to. Clarity. Dignity. All of what we have lost as humans is transparent in the eyes of one who lives from the Land. The tingling sensation returns in my face. It feels as if my face is elongating. I see you, Fox, and you are a child and a killer. You are bigger than I and you will have a better life and death. You are penetrating my body and changing my flesh with your eyes. Beckoning. You want me to Become with you.

No. Not yet. I am afraid. I collect my Wall and put it up between us. Fox scurries off towards another hole in the meshing. I follow my new friend. He will lead me to safety. Fox goes through the hole first, and abandons me. The hole is jagged and a lot smaller than the one I crawled through to get under the school. I am halfway out when my atigi cover tears. My mom is going to kill me. Attempting to rip the mesh into a bigger hole does not work because my mitts are hindering the dexterity of my fingers. I take them off to untangle my atigi from the metal and my fingers stick to the meshing for a second because of the nervous sweat on them.

Cold does not tolerate moisture in any form. I leave my skin behind. They are only cells. Any warm, wet surface will instantly freeze to metal. Children often find this out the hard way when they are very small, usually after one of their friends has dared them to stick their tongues onto the slide or swing set. The worst example of this I have ever seen was a kid with his tongue stuck onto a merry-go-round, and the other kids kept spinning and spinning him until he barfed. The warmth of the barf released his tongue and he went home sobbing. Poor kid. I've now almost freed myself from the mesh. Yes, there! Finally able to stand upright, I assess the damage to my atigi. The hole is fist sized, that's not too bad. Alpha and friends come around the corner just a second after the wind brings the dry crunch of their footsteps as a warning. This is the wrong type of snow for a good warning system. The wind was blowing in the wrong direction and did not deliver me Sound. Fuck.

I'm running. Hair in face, ice in lung, heavy of foot. Sometimes they are too slow to catch me. They usually can't keep up, because I run even faster than the boys. Today I wore my heavy Sorel boots instead of my kamiit and therefore I am slow. One of Alpha's cronies throws a rock and it strikes at the base of my skull. I fall.

I arrive home with a bloody nose and hair full of frozen phlegm. Spit freezes so quickly; it's a good punishment to get it into the hair. The hot shower is so good. All the evidence goes down the drain. I will not tell my parents about this. Parents let children work out their own social problems. I let the experience go down the drain with the water. No point hanging on to such things. Ultimately, in the scope of the universe, this is a small event. Trauma does not choose you, you choose if it is trauma or not, right?

Sleep has left me because "Born to Be Alive" is blasting in the living room. My feet hit the floor and the carpet feels extra pilly on my soles because of the depth of sleep my body was in. Damn drunks. Addiction is anything that feels good in the moment but ultimately makes you feel worse, a degeneration of the psyche that takes shape physically. All our weaknesses add up and become our strongest adversaries. It is fuel for self-hatred, insecurity, self-pity, and martyrdom.

Booze in belly,

Hollow of soul,

Impoverished of Morals,

Out of control

I look forward to the morning, when everyone is back to the people I love. A glimpse into the living room reveals ten people in the process of driving away their Protectors. This always seems like the goal. Get fucked up enough that the shell of who you are gets cast off, leaving room for who you don't want to be. There are evil beings in the room near the ceiling waiting to take over the drunken bodies, Grudges and Frustrations slobbering at the chance to return to human form, to violate, to kill, to fornicate; Old Spirits conniving and contriving more strife. Fuck this. I get dressed and sneak out of the house. When your body is clear there is control. When your body is clear you can choose whom to let in. There is love everywhere.

Please cradle my rabbit heart. Please navigate yourself around me well. I know too much. I can recognize darkness because he is my brother, my maker. I can drink lightness because it is the only way to survive. I can shut off my heart but that leads to evil, so I express her and revel in the nuance of blood currents, and the sacred demons. I fear and quake with my eyes darting fight or flight love or die. The lightning comes from below this time and rips out of my throat for the world to see. They all see my rabbit and I have trained her to hunt. In her perfect glory she is shy and extroverted, chaste and perverted, my sweet near-death more alive than ever. Take her. Take me while I am ripe and open, rub berries on my lips and bear fat in my hair. Tattoo me with a needle and impale me with your warmth. Heal me, fuck me, and work my heart till she beats strong and unafraid. Haunches bared, teeth sharpened, wide-eyed and aware. Hurry. I want to feel safe.

The Northern Lights are in the sky. It's not too cold outside. Sun comes out for hours at a time now, and eventually she will drive away the Northern Lights completely. I walk out onto the sea ice until the town is a small glowing orb on the horizon and lie down. The flat land and the flat ice make the Sky endless. They say time is relative. It is. Humans have misunderstood time. Time is not rushing by. Time does not obey the clock. Time obeys physical laws like matter does, but it can control matter as well. Time is Matter. Time is alive. Time is aware. Time has weight. Time mates with gravity to put you back into the earth. You do not travel through time; time travels through you, drives you. Time is your conductor; time is your demise. Time sleeps beside me as I lie on the surface of the ice to help my heartbeat slow and body temperature drop.

Peace enters me. As Body grows dormant, Spirit awakens. Body is so crude, viscous and lumbering. Spirit has learned to hibernate within the confinement of mucus and gristle. Our meat keeps Spirit occupied and distracted. Our electricity ensnares Spirit and our flesh entraps it. We will spend our lives trying to contemplate and encapsulate the divinity of Spirit, only to blunder forth and never relax into letting the Communication happen.

Our minds are our prisons. There are secrets hidden in our flesh. Our cells being born and dying with the same force that makes galaxies form and deconstruct. Context. Perspective. Scale. Our galaxy is a proton. We are everything. We are all and we are nothing. Everyone has the niggling sensation that we are missing something in this world, but I have the key.

The ice begins to beckon the heat from Body. As Body goes limp and Mind goes quiet, Spirit awakens and collects in my chest, using the energy and currents in wave and wind to generate strength. I push Spirit downwards, using Intention and Will to separate from and abandon Body. Body does not want Spirit to leave, for that normally means death. It takes a lot of calm coaxing, convincing, and contracting to have Body give Spirit permission to leave. Gently reassuring each cell that Spirit will return, I feel for an opening in the ice and find the smallest crack and slip into the Arctic water below. The water does not feel cold but feels like syrup; the viscosity of the water changes because Spirit moves through it differently than Body does. I want to look for Sedna but the current is strong, and if Spirit becomes lost Body will succumb to the cold.

I can hear all the algae; they are happy to see me. Rotating and celebrating, microbes twist and turn in Life Dance. Small shrimp and tiny organisms sing welcome and give thanks. Life pops forth brightly and death is a soft exhalation. They are not so much living and dying as glowing and darkening. There is no light without darkness and death is life. Spirit anchors a sinew-like rope onto Body and travels downwards to the ocean floor. The bottom of the ocean is like a stadium event of Life as I slowly spread myself out to hold and love as many creatures as possible. Spirit drinks from Life. This is the secret.

Spirit is already divine. We must feed Divinity with devout intent and Spirit grows stronger, cleansing and returning to reality upon Death. What happens before birth and resumes after death—this is more real than the brief spark of life. Our lives just carry the physical burden of carrying energy forward. We put on suits of meat as training, as a challenge. We all know this is temporary.

The ocean current calls to me and I realize that Body is slipping away. It takes every ounce of energy I have to travel back to the surface. It's laborious and very slow. For one terrifying moment I am trapped under the ice. The small crack lets me through and I get back up into my cold and dark casing. Ice in mouth, crack of vertebrae, and song in spleen. It takes a monumental effort to wiggle my toes and open my eyes after the Exploration.

The Northern Lights have descended upon me during my spirit journey. Fantastical and omnipotent, they were called forth by the Exploration. They noticed the activity. Shining brighter and clearer than I have ever witnessed, they came down in a mighty and cyclonic display of power. Mere metres above me, they sound like ancient whales and snapping ice.

The drone of their vibration is loosening my marrow. There is no time for Fear, because Fear is gnawing on one side of Body, but it has not yet reached my heart. Towering and sublime, the Northern Lights come closer. My eyelids are frozen open but Body grows warmer. I can't move. Light leaves Time and takes on physical form. The light morphs into faces and creatures, and then they begin to solidify into violent shards. This energy is not benign like that of the ocean dwellers; these are the Masters of Law and Nature. Fear beats Time to my heart and it beats faster and faster because I am powerless now.

The Light glows too hard. I'm blind. The Light shapes itself into long shards and attaches to the surface of my eyes. It burns worse than anything I have ever felt. Like the cold freezes moisture, the light seems to sear my fluid.

My nostrils begin to burn as the glow grows down my face and cheeks. I groan as it travels up my nose and into my sinus cavities. My ears become plugged and filled. The backs of my eyeballs begin to melt from agony to ecstasy as a large shard of light is thrust down my throat. I can't breathe for an

113

SPLIT TOOTH

instant but the panic melts as my throat is opened; it is slit vertically but not destroyed. I'm healed with torture.

The slitting continues down my belly, lighting up my liver and excavating my bladder. An impossible column of green light simultaneously impales my vagina and anus. My clit explodes and I am split in two from head to toe as the light from my throat joins the light in my womb and begins to make a giant fluid figure eight in my Body.

I am lifted off the ground and realize that this is the end of Life. Nobody can survive this. I can go forever now into the bliss. Join the light. Light in lung. Light in soul. Opening of holes.

Pain. I am naked and freezing. My skin almost tears off the ice as I stand up. My clothes are scattered around me. I am shaking violently. I put on my clothes and stagger home, bleeding from every orifice. My parents are at work. I was gone for twelve hours. A hot shower calms me and washes the shaking away. I can never tell anyone about this. Nobody would believe me. I wipe my pussy and green glow is left on the Kleenex. It squirms like a larva.

MISPLACED

My womb is impregnated with mourning
The past and I conceiving
Heaving
Birthing sorrow
Intangible currency
Misplaced kitchen knives
My sliced honour carries

A flag covered with bright colours
Steep cliffs want me
To pretend to have feathers
Hang your black hair over me
Not under
March your black boots
Over me
Not under
Blinking sawdust loud dry labour
I smell falsehood
I open my palms to reveal
An alley of sled dogs
Eating lies
I press my mouth to the ground
And join them

It's weeks later and I have told no one of that night. I told no one of the changes, the loosening of tendon and the tightening of muscle; the stitching of gristle and accelerated healing. My cuts heal in half a day. I no longer need glasses. I can see people's words before they come out of their mouths. My skin is clear. My eczema has disappeared. I have to clip my nails every other day now. There are deep shades of green in my eyes, my mom notices. She attributes it to puberty, since I am now finally developing substantial breasts. Am I taller, or do I just stand that way?

Strange things start happening. There is a shift in rituals. We kids used to sit in a circle and slice each other's names into our arms. We sliced with razor blades and made false claw scars to prove ourselves worthy of pain. I can no longer bleed from my wounds, even when we slice deeply. Blood wants to stay in my core now. The membranes around my organs thicken. My heart beats more slowly. Calmness replaces anxiety. The tips of my fingers taste like metal.

The scope of my vision expands. The bowl of my pelvis is filled with honey and my tongue is poisonous. I have learned to coax orgasms out of the sacred place and all of the fluid in the world is mine.

The sun rises in the morning now. Soon it will be the Time of Abundance. What a relief. It brings brightness of mind and body to be reassured that the cold will lose its mighty grip on us. Soon the snow buntings will arrive, bringing song. My favourite snow bunting song is the clearance song they make to land. On walks to school, I observe them and try to decipher their language. The chirps sometimes blur into words if I stop trying to listen. I realize that birds see in a completely different way than we humans do. We are slow and lumbering, our language is deep and muddy. Our confinement to the ground elicits pity. They look at us as we look upon the trees, slow but full of longevity. The trees look at the rocks that way. Rocks look at the mountains that way. Mountains look at the water that way. Earth looks at the sun that way. Everyone has an elder.

There is an old debilitated ship across the bay, a reminder of the many failed attempts foreigners made to claim the Northwest Passage. I have never understood why foreigners will imagine themselves extreme adventurers while the stewards of the land observe with a chortle. We have always been here. Aren't we adventurous? How presumptuous it is to assume that an experience is limited to your own two eyes.

It takes only fifteen minutes to walk across the frozen bay.
Now that it is bright and warm enough to stay outside with
comfort, we walk across almost daily. The ship is a source of
shelter when the winds pick up, and also a spark to ignite our
imaginations. Who was the captain? Did they cast any bodies
overboard? Had they succumbed to scurvy? Did they bring
tuberculosis? Did their lips retreat in agony from their teeth
as they received the same treatment the elements have always
given us? The Land has no hierarchy. The Land has no
manners; you only obey and enjoy what is afforded to you
by her greatness. Only logic and great care ensure your survival. Only the patterns of skills gifted by our ancestors
keep us living in harmony. We obey or we succumb.

Best Boy grips the frayed rope that hangs from the mast
and runs off the prow, swinging in a great circle around the
ship. He is silhouetted by the bright sky for a moment, and
gladness and laughter explode out of him and enter us all.
We take turns zipping through the sweet cold air and risking
the fall. Best Boy and I retreat into the belly of the ship to
meet our friends. He puts his cold hands under my jacket
and shirt. It's only common courtesy to warm the hands of
those you care for. Our friend is rabidly digging the snow
out of the belly of the ship, trying to excavate knowledge.
Curiosity is the crux of youth. He screams that he has found
hair, a buried head. We run, choosing to believe in the won-
derment and the fantasy, high on fear. When we finally return

months later, it turns out that the hair was just the ragged end of a rotted mop. In all our joviality, we had forgotten to apply logic. It was fun to believe we had found a body, considering that there was a real body of a shaman that had rotted at the town dump, rejected from the public graveyard by the Anglican ministers. I never understood how foreigners could come and tell us where to die and where to live. Where to be buried and how to breed.

Thrice placed lichens

In order

Lime green

Orange

Black

Three rows

Four regrets

Eight tears

Backwards whispers intact

Said quickly

Subliminally

Criminally

Move forward

Three lies

Four fists

Eight facts

Stones collected

Warmed by body

Warmed with life

Place them

In order

Hexagonally

Six enemies

Three curses

Four lovers

Eight pacts

Time has a way of eternally looping us in the same configura-
tions. Like fruit flies, we are unable to register the patterns.
Just because we are the crest of the wave does not mean the
ocean does not exist. What has been before will be again.
We are reverberations of our Ancestors and songs of our
present selves. It is very quiet in the future, as it is in the
deep past. The Quiet. We always live alongside the dead.
It's scary but the Quiet is our true home. This is why we
must make the most of our gristle and meat.

We must celebrate being harnessed into our bodies.
We are a product of the immense torque that propels this
universe. We are not individuals but a great accumulation
of all that lived before. They are with us. They lift us. We
will lift them later. We must use our sight for visions and
our touch for love. Feed our hands and feed our bellies.
Feed your eyes and feed your bones. We are vessels to be
filled, and I have felt renewed after the night on the ice.

My tendons are thicker, my thoughts quicker. I am more capable.

Fear is learning to run from me, not the other way around. I am not afraid anymore, as if meekness is slinking away into the deeper corners where it cannot dominate my psyche. The night with the Northern Lights changed my whole life. They say that the insane never doubt their own sanity. The night with the Northern Lights was real. The pain was real. This is where my lesson was learned: pain is to be expected, courage is to be welcomed. There is no choice but to endure. There is no other way than to renounce self-doubt. It is the time of Dawning in more ways than one. The sun can rise, and so can I.

My newfound confidence has drawn in more attention from Best Boy, but maybe it's just my breasts. We find any excuse to spend time together, even though we are awkwardly navigating our friendship. We break into abandoned buildings just to keep warm. We climb the oil tanks and run around the tops of them, daring ourselves to jump off (we never do). We challenge the power plant to a yelling match. We collect our friends in gangs and each one of us tells our parents we are sleeping over at someone else's house. We hold 100 metre races and play spin the bottle. We steal hash and beer and potato chips. We talk on the phone. We taunt drunks on the street, knowing they will never remember who bruised their egos when they have killed their own dignity already.

I am no longer shocked by Best Boy's ability to manipulate with his eyes. It now seems slightly amusing. I have no more uses for him other than friendship since discovering that he is so very funny. You never know where a true friendship will bloom. I'm aware that he tries to seduce me but know instinctively that it has nothing to do with me. I don't know how to break it to him that after the night on the ice, no one will ever penetrate my Self again. Hopefully he sees that I am more than pussy. He tries to treat me like sex but it is like water off a duck's back. He is so vulnerable, and this has led to fear. He acts out of fear.

Laughter is the fear killer. Nervous laughter when you feel awkward or embarrassed. Belly laughter when someone is inappropriately appropriate. Whispered giggles when people make fools out of themselves. Helpless sniggering at people who take themselves so very seriously. Milk shot out of your nose at your dad when he calls you a fart sack. Mostly the laughing at the ridiculous sideshow we call reality. This heals.

Alpha is not happy with the friendship between Best Boy and me. It is a school day and I am not hiding from her anymore. It doesn't matter what they do to me, today is the day I stand up for myself. No choreographed detention, no crawling under the school.

The time ticks by, and I know what awaits me. The bell rings. The walk to my locker seems to be happening in slow motion. It's the adrenaline. I walk out of the school with my books and there is a semicircle of girls waiting for me at the bottom of the stairs. Alpha is sneering and the others shift their weight from one foot to the other in anticipation.

There are waves of violence lapping around our legs. Everything is moving very slowly but seems to come into focus very easily. I exhale long like I'm aiming my rifle and step down into the semicircle. Even this small act of taking space is more defiant than anything I have ever dared to do before, and there is an almost imperceptible shift in power and movement as the semicircle takes a slight step back and goes quiet.

I collect all the energy from around me and focus it into my core, then up to my eyes. I wish that my best friend Battery Pack was with me, but I can do this alone. Alpha feints like a boxer and spits in my face.

I grab her scarf and quickly wrap it around her throat. She seems so light as I spin her around and lift her up off the ground by the weight of her neck. She can't breathe. She's turning red and her stupid little friend tells me to stop in a quivering voice.

I wait. I wait until she is purple and drop her. She is unconscious but she will be all right. They will never, ever bother me again. I am glowing light all the way from my spleen. As peaceful as I wish to be, it certainly feels good to get drunk on violence.

Gravel underfoot
Ice in lung
Drunk on fun
Drunk on violence
Drunk on cum

I will sharpen my claws

Bare my teeth

One saliva string

One tongue

Cannot speak of the

Fight that comes from survival

Touch my children

And my teeth welcome your windpipe

Utter the name

And be crushed by leg

Grown strong from

Holding up weight

By thigh that carries

Rocks and urgent gait

I will hunch my shoulders and wait

Claws sharpened

Teeth agape

School is finally out and the sun is permanently up. The twenty-four-hour sun is not conducive to mischief, since witnesses can view our actions plainly, whether it is midnight or noon. Our troublemaking intentions are revealed in the volume of our voices. Our need for mischief amplified by the midnight sun and lack of schedule. Everyone's clocks tick sideways. We stay up until noon and sleep until 8 p.m. because it doesn't matter.

In the Bright Night there are only the Alive people out, the young or drunk or those coming home from a hunt. We haven't quite outgrown throwing stones at drunkards and picking cigarette butts off the ground outside the Northern Store. There are four of us together today and Yellow Pants has stolen a joint off a drunkard after pelting stones at him, so we are set for the night. It's about two in the morning as we break into a small shed down by the shore, caribou hair and seal fat sticking to the bottom of our shoes. The door is stuck, frozen into a piece of ice. We force it from its ice prison and our eyes adjust to the dimness as the door closes into blackness. Blood and oil is a very comforting smell. Seal grease and matted fur. There is metal in the air from the snowmobile parts, and the smell of salt being released by the cracks in the ice. The thick oil is causing heaviness in our nostrils. Smelling gravel, dust, plywood, and concrete; we shuffle into the small enclosure.

A strange feeling washes over me, something predatory. I have caught the scent of fear. I can smell fear and it excites me. Bloodlust but more like Spiritlust. The fear talks to my teeth and wants them to grow large and pointed. The fear talks to my spine and tells it to be near to the earth, because you can hide your belly that way. The fear talks to my eyes and tells them to see food in the veins of necks. Something flips inside my tummy.

Someone sparks the joint. Instinct takes over and I direct my focus onto the weakest member of the group, Yellow Pants. He looks me in the eye for a second and starts to scream at the top of his lungs. He keeps screaming that he has seen the devil. I didn't mean to scare him THAT much, and now I feel petulant, as though the kill happened too quickly. We usher him out of the shack as people start to come to their windows to see what the ruckus is. He is rolling in the mud now, wet with seal blood and fat. I am simultaneously regretting the situation and laughing internally at him, disgusted by his weakness. He won't stop screaming.

Finally his mother comes to pick him up. We stand around, sheepish, concerned and embarrassed. Why was he so afraid? Did he not know that fear attracts predators? He was never the same after that.

Neither was I. The Land started to call more often after that. The Land soaks up the guilt stubbornly clinging to my liver after using another person as prey, for my own enjoyment. The Land soaks up all negativity. Breathing with the Land, giving energy back into the earth, that is survival. Plug my body into the nuna and soak her up, give her back love. A universe-sized love encapsulated in a moment, in a breath, a gift for my impoverished flesh. She is all-encompassing. She is peaceful. She is sublime. We will all be back in the earth soon, why not enjoy being outside of her now?

After death my body rot is the newborn of inanimate objects. Maybe the earth misses our bodies the way a mother misses a newborn. Maybe we miss our bodies the way we all miss the womb when we're dead. Maybe my minerals will come back quickly as a plant or insect. Maybe parts of me will become the Old Blood in millennia, the Old Blood we suck out of the earth to burn and destroy the surface, to burn and eviscerate the clouds. Leave the blood in her. Let the deep black of time stay where it belongs. Compressed and ancient, we force the Old Blood to work in the wrong time, at the wrong pressure.

What happens to the energy once it leaves our body?

Does it leave us or does it start vibrating at an unknown frequency? Does it cast itself into the wind and leave our vessels lonely? Do our spirits travel with the wind? Do our spirits retain our value and ascend into the Knowing or are we demoted when our bodies decay? Are we as worthy while we rot? How many layers of consciousness are there? Are we still giving? Is being inanimate really a lesser state?

I think not. It is just a slower state. Is the air more enlightened than we are? Land always answers these questions for me. Land protects and owns me. Land feeds me. My father and mother are the Land. My future children are the Land. You are the Land. We destroy her with the same measured ignorance of a self-harming teenager. That is what I was in my fifteenth year, what is your excuse? I want to save the land as much as my mother wants to save me.

I haven't had my period since the night on the Ice. I have not told anyone about the flipping in my belly because my tummy has stayed flat. All I know is that I am not alone anymore; I am protected now. The melt had the last of the snow running in rivers and the melt has blood pooling around my womb.

This is the time of Growth, of prosperity. Goodness has filled the bellies of the hungry. Rich thick fresh meat creates perfect shining strength. Small purple flowers have bloomed and blossomed in patches all over the tundra. Arctic poppies invade the land like small armies. Aigaq roots are kicked from their flowers and find themselves in bellies. The land is flush with animals.

Fox visits me often, but he treats me with a different reverence and would never dare talk to me again now that I have the twins in my belly. I speak with the twins every day, a boy and a girl.

I am filled. They are always pulling at me, playing with me and telling me what to eat. They often want me to leave my consciousness and come to them into our spirit world where we can communicate freely. We laugh like old people having tea when I am with them in our mind's eye. My elders are in my tummy. I respect and admire them. They know so much more than I do. No one else knows about them because they move like fast snakes in my stomach. They are not my children but my equals and my leaders.

Children always need direction. Of course they do. But only in how to stay alive. If we trust their wisdom, they will know how to conduct themselves in a true sense. At some point these beings will have to evacuate themselves from my body. What will I tell my parents? I am still their baby, their baby that likes to search. I am their baby that dreams in a sick horror of the exploding pleasure of the Northern Lights. I am the baby of tingling breasts and swollen desire.

Best Boy picks me up most evenings to go for a walk because quite frankly sometimes it's the only thing to do. The sun brings us around the periphery of the town; we are scuffing and meandering, saying nothing. Sometimes it feels like this town is a still-water lake and there is no wind. No air. We will suffocate if we are not careful. We stop and sit on a rock and let the sun speak. I love to sit and watch Best Boy breathe. I love catching his scent on the wind. A hint of breath, a hint of old laundry, fresh skin.

He is almost motionless. I love seeing his old-man eyes when we are alone. He lets himself be calm and old when we are alone. We could be alive now, we could be a thousand years ago, but we cannot be a thousand years from now because this land will have changed, drowned, unearthed, burned, and hopefully begun reassembling after we humans are gone.

We pick back up after a long time to continue our search for nothing. Music comes out of some homes, suicide out of others. We see our dorky little friend peering out the bedroom window of a house blasting country music. Seems festive. It's early enough, so we risk going inside and try to be as invisible as possible as we pass the adults in the living room.

We almost go unnoticed when a drunkard stops us with a loud "HEY! KIDS, COME HERE." We sheepishly inch over into the circle of bleary eyes. He simply hands us a large container of Player's Light tobacco, some pre-made paper and filter tubes, and a cigarette-making machine. "Go make me smokes."

We happily oblige. Sitting in a circle of three, we enjoy the time together, getting sticky fingers from learning how much or how little tobacco to pack into the machine before we take the paper tubes and slide the empty ends onto the metal holders and push the tobacco in with a satisfying click. We smoke all the cigarettes that we make a mess of. We inhale all of the superfluous tobacco like it's a fountain of adulthood.

Watching the smoke curl under the rim of my ball cap while I puff and ash without using my hands makes me feel like I'm good at something, it makes me feel like I'm a grown-up. We pretend to be accountants, gangsters, Clint Eastwood. Hours pass and we discuss minutiae but in reality we measure fortitude. We take our leave out the window when the party gets louder, abandoning our little friend. My arm hooked through Best Boy's, we walk through town and allow the whispers to follow behind us. Being followed by whispers is better than being led by screams.

There is little weight in my belly but I am much heavier now. Everyone thinks it's puberty. An old woman named Helen approached me in the store today and invited me out to her tent to have tea. I have always known her, just as all of us in our small community have known each other. I often see her at the Bay or Co-op, collecting supplies for bannock. She is known for her coil bannock, though I have never tasted it.

She is the grandmother of Best Boy, and I know she senses him on me. Her crinkled face shows only a shadow of the power she owns, only what she chooses to show. Humility surrounds her, but we all revere her. I think she senses something more than I can possibly observe. Her hands hold the wisdom of a thousand years.

Her skin is loose and thin, but the gristle of her is visible even through her softness of age. She is formidable, and you must not show her your self-doubt. She will tire of you and leave. It's the blackness of her eyes. Looking at her brings a deep calmness, but the torment of her memories stirs a deeper urgency. She needs something from me. I can help her. She can help me.

I watch her waddle away; the wolverine fur on the hood of her coat is so dark next to the whiteness of her hair. The majesty of thinning grey has somehow managed to conquer the dark, oily thickness of the fur. She is the queen of the unseen. Her body is heavy but she moves with light and the energy around her swirls like a slow tempest. The air around her shimmers like a heat wave. Her body is ruined by time but her true self sashays with the slow roll of a woman's pelvis when the uterus is full. She does the best sewing, her family adorned like royalty with her stitches. Richness. The woman is like marrow on the tongue. To hunger for energy that is outside of food, outside of sex, and outside of violence; this is peace. This is safety.

Tuesday evening I venture with my dog out onto the tundra.
The summer night is dusty and dry. The clouds make patterns
that look like a Morse code warning: The summer will not
last. This is life. Eat it now. My dog's fur is cream and salmon
coloured, his eyes so pale that they mimic the whitecaps.
Everyone is afraid of him because he is so large but we know
each other, and he makes this nature complete.

After hours of walking we come upon a lake, and we
decide it's time to cool off. He gets into the water first.
I remove all of my clothing and stand in the sun, calf deep
in clean lake. I don't feel like a young girl anymore. I am a
woman now. I settle into the water and let the cold support
me. The waves lap up against stomach and shoulders as
I watch the light dancing all over the water. See the reflection
of the clouds? See my dog lapping up the freshness?

I put my head under the water for as long as I can. I am
pure. This baptism does not belong to Christians. This
baptism belongs to the Land. I prop myself up on my elbows
and let the waves put their hands around my throat.

All of a sudden I am thirsty. Very, very thirsty. Too thirsty.
Small fish and shrimp begin to collect like a halo around
my body. I open my legs wide and let water flow into me.
It doesn't stop. She is thirsty too. All the shrimp and fish
decide to follow, and she is less hungry. It feels like she is

swallowing little warm lights. A large char swims up too, bright orange and majestic. He is visible from afar and swimming very quickly. I am frightened because I am sure he will not fit. He swims in forcefully but I open like an accordion so it does not hurt. I close my legs as the bright warmth travels up my whole body. My children rejoice and consume. It tickles. My dog is laughing at me. I get dressed slowly, satisfied and selfish. We laugh together all the way home, my dog and I. Secrets are delicious.

Helen and I begin to visit more often. She never speaks to me about my pregnancy but she often offers me bone marrow, soup and tea. She speaks Inuktitut a lot of the time and slowly it penetrates my consciousness. I begin to dream in Inuktitut and my babies flutter with happiness when they notice my contentment. I am so connected with my growing babies that they have become individuals to me. One is soft and strong as the womb she lives in, the other has harder edges and wants to throw stones. One is smaller, meeker. The other protects her. The other is the opposite one. One is so bright and fragile she feels like an egg yolk in my tummy. The jagged one surrounds her with metal and mettle. I do not play favourites, though one induces pride and the other awakens my desperation to give care. I am aware that they cannot exist without each other, that they are the same person in different bodies. It's a pity they could not simply merge into one.

These babies have made me older. It is difficult to care about what I used to care about. Drugs make me feel sick. Booze makes me feel sick. Even cigarettes make me ill. Huffing gas makes me feel like I'm committing a crime. The cute boy doesn't hold my gaze any longer. He holds my hand. He holds my need for companionship. My eyes blur and look past him whereas before he shone like the sun. No one dares to enter my room at night. I can feel the crazed beasts that are resting in me, ready if I need protecting. I feel the deep centre of warmth that placates the beasts with love, because love must always lead. Through my babies I wordlessly speak with the past; through baby boy I speak with a quiet and serene old man that keeps an eye on the horizon to make sure the world spins properly on its axis. Through baby girl I speak to a giant female wolf that stalks the periphery of our territory to detect predators. Both are silent, but who needs words to speak when all is already known?

The twenty-four-hour sun is waning into long sunsets and bouts of twilight. The orange light is my favourite, slanted sideways and feeding my whole body. Hours of orange sunset spark long narratives and peel away the fear of accepting circumstance. My babies have become my obsession and they have completely taken over my body. I am no longer the driver of my movements or actions, and can no longer hide my stomach. When asked who the father is, I say nothing.

My own father is infuriated. I saw his eyes cloud over and saw that he would never love me in the same way again. He withdrew into himself and never came out again. I no longer have access to his love.

My mother accepted the pregnancy and tried her best to be supportive. She rubbed my back like I was still her little girl and sometimes I can hear her muffled weeping from the other room. They worked so hard to raise me right. I think they are looking for a place to lay blame, but are aware that there is no blaming the rain from under the awning. There are only facts.

I drink in the orange sun every night, and we all absorb the silence. Our house has become quiet, devoid of music. The parties become less joyous. Then the parties stop. A deep shame and reverence lies in the eyes of my parents when they look at me. I overcompensate by making too many jokes and being too loud. I can win their love back. I know it. It's not their fault that the lights took me. My babies will repair the damage. I can be their baby and have babies too. Acceptance and silence are carried and handed over to the orange sun. I hope my parents will be calm and learn to carry me again. I need them.

Heavy hands
Cupped palms
Carrying warm clear liquid
Slippery fingers
Let me undo your braid
Let your black hair cascade
Down your smooth brown back
Wood smoke and silence
Words not welcome

Let me comb your hair
Let the wind howl
Let me count your memories
Let me penetrate your warmth
With the rhythm of the brushstrokes
Let me smell the top of your head
Inhale your ideas
Let me braid your hair
Thick black
Raven feather black
Hear the elastic snap
I am in your braid now
You are in control
You just don't know it yet

After all the months of brightness we have our first shy nights of darkness. We have missed the darkness. My babies crave the night. I realize they are craving their Maker. They cannot see their father in the light. The darkness pulls my stomach outwards and downwards. They slither inside but sometimes remain perfectly still until I begin to grow concerned for their safety. They sense my agitation and wiggle around just to placate my worries. I have never felt so full.

The call of the moon is the calling of my uterus. I can feel the tides pulling under the ice. The water in me is pulled with it. The babies' faces always turn towards the moon. They are not normal babies; they are Fluid. I feel them growing legs, then shrinking and absorbing legs. They grow tails and fuse them together only to tear them apart again just for fun. They are one just like I dreamt they would be.

Their skin joins and separates at will. How will this be explained when they arrive? Sometimes they get angry at each other and flatten themselves on opposite sides of my uterine wall. This causes me great discomfort but it never lasts long. They get lonely very quickly and reach for each other at the exact same time. They dream the same dreams. I know because they thrash while sleeping in the exact same ways. Just like how the Northern Lights mirror each other on each pole, my children are not two, they ARE one.

It's the first of the long dark nights. We go walking on the sea ice in the hope that the children will meet their Maker. The Northern Lights are out and dancing but they do not notice us. I realize that bringing them out on the ice was a mistake when one of my children starts moving and writhing to the exact same rhythm of the Northern Lights. The babies came from the sky; it does not surprise me that they might want to return to it.

The boy starts to press against the inside of my cervix. He is curious. His sister clutches him and observes from behind, but certainly would follow him in an instant if he left my womb. I do not want to lose them just yet. It is my first time being whole. I do my best to calm the excitement and keep them in my belly. Deep breathing. We waddle home and I soothe them with promises of fish soup and warm tea. My breasts started to ooze a bright green and viscous liquid.

My milk.
Milk in breast,
Full of womb,
Close to tomb.

Knowing that the babies want to appear soon, I begin
to arrange the ceremony that will afford them the most comfortable birth. Instinct dictates that they not be birthed
amongst many people but must be born on the land. They
must spill forth onto five caribou skins, forty-two smooth
stones, eleven ptarmigan stomachs, eight human teeth,
and a flask of eighteen-year-old whisky. They must first see
someone who can be trusted. Helen. We need Helen to
facilitate the birth. My mother asked to be present, but she
cannot tolerate seeing me in pain. I want Helen. The children
want Helen because they have smelled the clean dryness
of her hands through my nose. They have looked upon her
from the top of my head. They have penetrated her thoughts
already. I hope the babies will come on a night of the Deep
Cold. Being pregnant makes me too hot.

The babies tell me two days beforehand that their Maker
will arrive to help them out of the womb. I desperately hope
that the Northern Lights will not simply take them from
me and up into the sky. These babies are mine too. Celestial
custody.

I go out to Helen's camp in the daytime and tell her that
I will come back in two days and bring dinner. She already
knows what is coming. I spend the next two days preparing
a feast. I spend the next two days focusing on my cervix and

collecting stones. It's scary. I don't know what birth will be. I want to dig into the centre of the earth. I want to mourn. I want to preen and gather, rinse and slather myself in oil. I put both hands in my vagina. She opens and blooms. I have three orgasms. The babies suck up the joy. We glow. I prepare fresh arctic char head soup and bannock, and caribou broth with rosemary for the birth. I will bring raw meat to fry and a few books to read.

Spirit to Flesh.
Ice in Lung.
Seed in Soil.
Precious Ones.

My small one. Her breath, her smile, and the smell behind her ears. I celebrate her tears, her eye twitch, and her wet mouth. I celebrate her movement, her hips, and her patellae. I celebrate her voice, out of tune and earnest. I am her creator, her home, and her comfort. I drink her tears and am her love, hate, and earth in one. I am her nurturer and provider, her nest and her shackles. I am her flesh and her bones, her fluids are mine and mine are hers. My small one. My growing one. My truly mine. Her laughter, and her certain uncertainty. Her realness, her spark, her anger and her trust. My earth monster, my celebration. Today is for her, and for me for choosing to make her, to keep her, and to love her.

The birth night arrives and I meet Helen at her camp. She had known what needed to be done and had asked her nephew to build us an igloo. This is a welcome break from the canvas tent we had been visiting in. I DO love the smell of the canvas and the flapping of the tarps in the wind, but an igloo is heavier and quieter. The entrance to the igloo is slightly larger than normal and a small ice window is placed directly on the side so we can sense the sky. The sleeping area is lined with caribou fur.

We are relaxing and drinking tea. We eat the food that had been prepared with the most Love. I observe the lines on her face, see the hang of her lip, the moisture within her. For a moment I can see her the way Cold sees warmth. Her fluids must be slowed and stopped. She must be preserved. I realize that Cold is not evil. Cold just doesn't like rot. Cold doesn't like change. Cold wants things neat and tidy, and our passionate and heated state simply does not coincide with Cold's frugal nature. Cold wants to clean us up by sopping up our

life and bringing us to his state. Cold wants to halt Time, halt our aging process, halt our movements, and halt our rot.

Helen and I are not going to go there tonight. Helen's lips are quivering a little bit, as if she is about to say something but decides not to. She inhales a shallow breath instead. Her eyes are in a slight state of panic, simply from absorbing the intention of my visit. Yet this woman remains calm. This woman could hold the breadth of the world on her lap if she desired. The steam comes up from our tea and I watch her hands fold around the cup. Her nails are slightly yellow but very thick. Her white hair is held back in a braid. I can tell there is a vast peace within her, but the years of holding back words have eroded her spirit. This woman has seen much. She has a network of scars on the tops of her hands. When I ask how she got them, the sides of her mouth curl up almost imperceptibly but she says nothing. I can see by her expression that it is not a pleasant story, and therefore not a good time to tell it. Now is the time for good stories, for nurturance and silence.

"Can we sleep here?" I ask. The same quiet smile appears. She shuts off the lamp and we lie under the caribou-skin blankets. The kullik still burns, and the smell of seal oil permeates everything. Helen lies beside me and her soft form feels so comforting, as if she were a blanket and a mountain at the same time. Her arm rests against mine and it feels so warm and sweet. As we lie together in silence, Helen opens herself to a half sleep. In her vulnerable state, her past begins to unravel behind her, and the shift of her tectonic plates reveals a gentle and bright young woman. Her road was clear, and then all of a sudden a knotted darkness appeared ahead. I saw on her path that she had committed a murder before. Someone had hurt her little sister, so she had killed him and told everyone that he had accidentally drowned. She pushed him out of a boat and into a fish net, only to let him drown. She watched him die with total detachment. His face mere centimetres from the surface, she calmly watched him stop twitching. THIS is why she is here; this is why she can see into my children and me. Those who have taken life of their own species can truly see into the spirit world, because the spirit of the deceased stays with you unless you eat their liver. She is more than strong enough to handle what is about to happen with this birth. The man she killed is watching us, but he is benign. He loves her now, as much as she still despises him. She swats at him like a fly to get him to leave her alone. Perhaps she regrets killing him, but it's always nice to have company. I observe her past and walk through it with her. She has always known mine. I know she hopes that my children will come out looking like her grandson. I'm going to be sorry to have to disappoint her.

If you are living in silence

With violence in your bones

Sorrow in your marrow

Blood running cold

Heal I beg you

Heal I beg you

Heal I beg you

Heal

The night sky starts to vibrate. Out through our little window the Northern Lights begin to thrum. My uterus tightens. The babies wake up and begin to wiggle excitedly. I know that the birth time is near because of the plugging of my ears and the pressure on my chest.

Helen has been sleeping, but she lets out a sigh and rolls over to face me. Her eyes are full of warmth and slumber and they connect with mine. The love from her is truly a gift. Even though I am full of fear, she puts her hand on my face and gives calmness to me. She sits up and starts to sing her pisik song, and boils some water. The lamp gets lit. The Northern Lights are growing stronger. As the Northern Lights grow, my fear shrinks.

My mouth wants to open, so I open it and let out a small string of noise. The sound started as a vibration from my children and travelled up my esophagus. I am not surprised to see a thin green string of light flow out of my mouth and float upwards. The Northern Lights notice it and grow sharper. They are coming. The green brightness eclipses the lamp and the igloo begins to fill with sharp shadows. My babies begin squirming faster and faster. They feel like a hundred fast snakes writhing in unison, and my stomach ripples like it is going to burst.

My face has grown flushed. I was expecting pain. I was expecting something other than feeling like the moon had grown fingers and used them to coax open my cervix. There was only a slight pinching inside. Suddenly my Uterus tightens and reminds me that I am the conduit from the spirit world into the physical one, and that Death wants me as much as Cold does.

My water breaks and flows out of me in a great river, bright green sparkling liquid. The liquid flows upwards and evaporates the ice window, allowing the string from my mouth to finally attach to the Northern Lights outside. The Northern Lights come down into the igloo and cover my body like a blanket. This experience is the exact opposite of the last one; a gentle warmth and love pours forth. The lights are softer this time. The Northern Lights wrap behind my head to help me be comfortable and roll down my belly to placate the babies.

The babies become calm and have decided now is the time to come and meet their Maker. The Northern Lights enter my mouth and my vagina while closing my anus and colon to make more room. My uterus hardens and forces

and pushes. The Northern Lights have robbed my mouth
of sound and my vagina of constriction.

I cannot see over my belly but I hear Helen scream as
my son Savik slips out of me. Wet and warm. Painless. Not
just painless, but pleasant. The Northern Lights are pleasur-
ing me during birth! Naja comes out next, free and sweet.
I sit up to look at my children and see why Helen is screaming. Both my children are each almost three feet long and
not much thicker than their umbilicus. They did not want
to hurt their mother, so they changed form at the direction
of the Northern Lights. My heart bursts with love. They are
covered in green slime and pulsating, but they are the most
beautiful things I have ever seen. Savik is much larger than
Naja. Both of them emit a sound at the exact same time that
cracks the sky open and sounds just like electricity. A flash of
lightning comes out of their mouths and joins the Northern
Lights in a snap so loud Helen stops screaming. Each of their
umbilical cords breaks free from their bodies and shoots into
each of Helen's eyes. She freezes and remains motionless,
mouth hanging open. The umbilicus is bloodied and so
are her eyes, but I have a premonition that it will work
out just fine.

I feel the umbilicus search her mind for the memory of
their birth. The cords suck the memory out of her consciousness and replace it with a more plausible birthing memory.
It takes a few minutes for this to happen. Helen is eerily still

and silent. Meanwhile my children have fleshed out into normal-looking newborns and the Northern Lights drift out and off into the sky, leaving us in darkness. The umbilical cords return to my children, and by the time Helen opens her eyes they have attached back onto the babies' bellybuttons. Cold has put the ice window back. Helen moves quickly to place my children onto my chest, and both of them begin to suckle from my breasts. Helen looks dazed but intact. We laugh; she wipes the sweat from my brow. The circle of life is complete as the milk flows out of me. Astounding green milk.

There is a celebration when we bring the babies home. People come over and bring food. Auntie brings fresh muqtak and uujuq. There is baked char, fried char, frozen char, and dried char. The caribou is roasted with blueberries and qungaliq juice. Another auntie made a potato salad and pumpkin pie. The soup is boiling and the bannock frying. Everyone is eating and laughing and cooking. My mother instantly fell in love with the babies, but my father remains distant.

Savik is very fat with a thick bunch of black hair and sharp features. His eyes are the darkest black and his skin is like teak. When he stares into your eyes, you can feel the sharpness of his thoughts. He is a natural protector. Naja is considerably smaller with no hair. No eyebrows, no fuzz. Even her eyelashes are stunted. Her features are softer than her

brother's, her nose rounder, her skin is darker and her eyes are
a very dark green instead of black. She is an abyss. It is so easy
to fall into her. She is sweet. Always cooing. Savik is silent.
The Knowing in his eyes is alarming. He makes sound only
when you keep him from Naja for too long, then he releases
a piercing cry until he is reunited with her. Naja is social and
soft. She rarely cries for her brother but gets agitated when
Savik is calling her to him. She obeys him. I can see it. He is
also her servant.

Savik has a natural electromagnetism around him. People
seem to become transfixed by him. Almost hypnotized. He is
pointed, brooding. When anyone holds him they begin to feel
uncomfortable after a few minutes. They begin to churn and
need a way to get rid of all the energy. I have noticed that
people can only hold him for so long before starting to say
disparaging things about other people. If they hold him even
longer they might cry in mourning or in grief. Savik eats
up the agony, and seems to grow stronger when he bears
witnesses to suffering. It's a relief for people to release their
troubles, but troubles must emerge when they are ready to.
Forcing out that agony leaves an open wound, it leaves people
depleted. I notice that those who spend too much time with
him grow ill and radiate a grey pallor.

I notice how he can control his environment. He can
use a glance to make someone fall down the stairs, or he
can go into people's minds and convince them to make

terrible decisions. You would think these things would make me dislike him, but they don't. They make me proud to have made such a source of power. A mother cannot control the love she has for her children. Mine is cyclonic. Savik never uses his will against mine. He is incapable of doing so. It would be like cutting himself.

Savik dislikes people, and my uncle in particular. In fact, my uncle even turns a little bit green when he is holding Savik. I wonder what it is inside of my uncle that keeps bringing him back to Savik; perhaps he carries guilt and enjoys revelling in it. It seems that Savik mostly preys upon men, but he will drain a woman that is malevolent or carries too much grief. No one notices these imperceptible things, but I can feel it. I can feel Savik calling to him people that hold a lot of negativity. He tells the pain to grow. He likes to be held by those he can hurt easily. He magnifies their ugliness and pain, just because he enjoys it. They seem inexplicably drawn to him. This kind of life thrives off dying. It is predatory. Leave it to humans to find a way to hunt themselves. This life thrives on taking from one another. This type of life is the opposite of empathy. This is destruction. This is chaos. This is so satisfying.

Naja is so small and slight. She is merely half the size of Savik, her little face barely bigger than a fist. She is bright even when she is sleeping. She is calm and soft. Her voice heals anxiety, and plants want to grow towards her. She weaves peace from thin air. She inhales trouble and exhales solutions like a filtration system. She cleans people. She sees too much. Cruel people are not comfortable with her, because their impoverished way of thinking is denounced by her countenance. I saw her healing my mother's cold on a molecular level. She literally boosted her immune system. She feeds from my right breast, because it makes her holy milk. Savik feeds from the left; I make his iron milk. My left breast becomes much larger than my right because he eats so much more. There must be an imbalance of pain in the world.

A collective shift of consciousness

Is needed so

The sunflowers will all turn

Towards the sun

We would do anything for acceptance

Water Food Air Love

Approval

What drives a social climate?

We just do what the others do

Following

They say there is safety in numbers

Depends who is counting

They say it's wrong

They say it's right

Objective observation

Critical thinking

While we

Eat our puke

Off of a residential school

Dining room floor

Off of the floor of a porn set

Facial punishment all around

A collective shift of consciousness

Because sunflowers don't turn to the moon

Salting soil

Reaping sweat

Make those children work

For their misery

A collective shift of consciousness

Is needed

Before the sunflowers burn

161

We spend the next few months in isolated love. All of our corners are filled with grace. The children grow and Naja seems to be catching up to her brother's weight. He is typically rough, but all his edges become smooth when he touches his sister. They sleep as if they are in the womb, and instinctively understand that they have to act like any human until we are alone and the house is silent.

They sleep in a yin-yang position. Their bodies melt into each other. Sometimes they morph and intertwine with each other while they feed at my breasts. Little fingers wrapping around each other like new shoots. Sometimes his legs become hers, or her arms become his, and I have to send a message of caution through my milk. Someone may awaken in the house, and it takes time to untangle limb from limb. We must let no one see, but everyone knows. They know deep inside. There are others like this in the world, and everyone always knows. Nature loves to bring forth life. Nature loves women. Nature hopes to heal by creating the crest of this wave of life, but what happens when the ocean turns sour?

To feed is to love. I'm very proud of my milk. Each day the children grow stronger. The visitors have trickled down to a few here and there. Best Boy is one of them; he comes over with Helen to visit the babies. I admit that the babies begin to look like him a little, but they morph as they please. After all, Best Boy is the human male that sees them most often. It's unsurprising that they have taken the affection into their faces. They know the world needs to see a father in their faces.

It's imperceptible to anyone else, but I watch them absorb and mimic the movements and characteristics of those around them. Savik starts to look like my uncle on my father's side when he spends time with them. When Best Boy holds him, I witness the molecules and atoms shift with each breath. They inhale the exhalations of those holding them. They use the scent to navigate their past, their ancestry. They inhale your scent. They gauge how much to grow, how much to talk.

Savik seems to favour men and Naja seems to prefer women. She has begun to look mostly like my mother's side of the family, more fair and wide of shoulder. My mother loves her and my father has warmed up to the babies now.

Naja blooms everywhere she goes. She brings sheen to people's hair and glow to their cheeks. I watch people calm and loosen when she is near. She gives with abandon and Savik is very protective of her, as if he sees her healing as a waste of energy, energy that could be directed towards him. Energy she could be using to build a shield to protect herself from those that would take too much. He is greedy for her. She generates healing and then feeds from the happiness. In return, Savik filters pain for her. I hope that she does not break once she knows its barbs. Shielded from agony, she grows and feeds the moon. Feasting on frustration, he tunnels into the sun.

We spend a lot of time with Helen, in her home. It's a wonderful and warm home, always bustling with family. The scent of the roasting caribou, the sounds of the boiling seal meat, the sizzle of bannock frying in Crisco. Home sounds. Peace sounds. Safety sounds. We use a piece of cardboard on the floor as a table for feasting when there is a great raw chunk of frozen meat to be shared. A magnetic strip is bolted to the kitchen wall to hold the uluit. The sound of the uluit being sharpened always gave me a shiver. Metal on metal is a disturbing sound.

Her house is always meticulously clean and organized. Someone is always playing cards. There is a cribbage board carved from a walrus tusk. There is a walrus penis in the corner, a baleen tooth on the mantel. There are five spirits, three children, and two goldfish here today. Thimbles and needles are restless. Nobody smokes but there is an ashtray on the coffee table just in case. An old aunt with jutting shoulder blades rests in the back room with a pillowcase

full of memories and the hands of her dead husband holding
her head up.

The floors creak. The bathtub is stained brown from
the hard water. A tile is broken in half in the corner of the
bathroom. The doors are hollow. The spirits like to rest there.
Her great collection of photos is chronologically arranged
and stored in cardboard boxes. Prized photos of loved ones
are framed and arranged on the Family Wall. The CB radio
is always on so that we can keep track of the travellers and
hunters. Helen has plastic plants because she doesn't like to
water real ones.

She has an affinity for country music and likes to play the
accordion. The kids get up and jig when she plays, her stubby
fingers playfully expelling bright songs. The couches have
broken springs but the kids keep on jumping anyways. No one
bothers to reprimand them. The old brown floral patterning
has worn away on a few of the cushions. The armrests show
sad, peeking two-by-fours studded with staples. I get some
pliers and dig them out. No sense having one of the kids
hurting themselves.

The rug is a thick muddy orange to balance out the dark
wood-printed panelling. There are ten dried ptarmigan stomachs hanging from the ceiling like Christmas ornaments.
A television lurks in the corner, but no one turns it on. There
is no point. This space is too peaceful to pollute with the
electric jazzer. Electronics do not work well around the twins

165

SPLIT TOOTH

anyways. The mechanics begin to sputter and sometimes die with my children around, depending on the mood they are in. When they fight it's best to keep them away from each other. Savik is the only person that Naja will bear ill will towards, so when it comes it is too powerful, even for him. I have not had to punish them as of yet, but I wonder how I will go about the task. Should I ask their father?

The babies have begun to move. It's all I can do to reprimand them when they show their true colours and move too quickly or deftly. I don't want anyone to know what they are, and to be honest most people don't trust their eyes enough to see. Cognitive dissonance. I'm very proud of my new ones, who seem to teach me new levels of love every day. My flesh has been fulfilled. It is mostly the milk, the milk that astonishes me. I can feel my body producing the exact nutrients each child needs, but also it carries information that cannot be explained. It flows with murmured reassurances and whispered messages of encouragement for my children. I send knives and blades of protection to my children through my milk. I send the power to their white blood cells and deconstruct negativity for them. Savik grows sharp. My milk is a whetstone for his lacerating blade. He is vengeance. He is divine.

Naja grows deeper than I could have imagined. I watch the molecules grow in my children, and it is a perfect extension of them being inside my belly. They are still inside me, but outside. We are our ancestors. The spiritual umbilicus is apparent to all. The dead look upon us with the pure love of a mother's gaze. But the dead love us even more because of our flawed flesh and eternal confusion. The removal from form allows for total and complete unconditional love. We carry our dead with us like helium balloons. There is no breaking the umbilicus. I have seen this before. I have known my children before. They have always been with me. They are me. Loneliness does not exist.

Best Boy comes to his grandmother's house often. He loves my children. Everyone thinks he is their father but both of us know that we have never had sex. It seems the town, my parents, and everyone else has been placated with the idea of Best Boy being the father. If they want to think that, I certainly don't mind. My heart knows I will never truly belong to another after being with the Northern Lights. There was no corner of me unexplored, unsalvaged, or unused. The Northern Lights will know me always. Best Boy asks me how the children could possibly look so much like him. I say he and I look alike anyways. He breathes out as I breathe in and our hearts beat at the same time. The babies call to him. We laugh like children should laugh and he helps me remember that I am still a child. Sometimes I ask him why he is so interested in my babies and me. He says we are magic. He says that he was bored before. He likes the laughter.

Uncle sinks further and further into sickness after spending time with Savik. He is my favourite uncle and it pains me to see him weaken. He holds Savik for comfort but it is the root of his demise, much like an addiction. Naja and I watch Savik travel into Uncle's body to help the sickness grow. I want him to stop but we all know that controlling the foundation of our children's nature is an act of futility.

I remember in fondness the time my uncle pulled me from a crack in the ice after a dangerous misstep. He saved me. I remember the times he gave me the best pieces of meat. I remember the time he was drinking with my parents and told my dad to be fair when disciplining me. He is soft. He has heavy eye bags and a resonant voice. The pitch of his voice demands that others quieten when he speaks. When he tells stories people's shoulders relax with calmness or tense with anticipation. He wears old clothing, mostly outdoor gear. Bespectacled and mostly quiet, he becomes loud and dangerous if drunk. I saw him take down three men in a fight over a woman. His humour can disarm anyone. The divide between gentle and malevolent is wide.

My heart hurts for him and Savik knows it. Savik doesn't care about my feelings, and for the first time I experience a removal from him. He acts on his own accord and it frightens me. Uncle's frequent trips to the nursing station get him medevaced out for testing. There is no hospital here. We have to leave town by plane to be treated. The tests reveal that he has a liver tumour that cannot be operated on; it has grown and attached to a main artery. He chooses to come home to die. I watch Savik suck his entire life out of him with a carnivorous glee. He grows stronger as Uncle grows weaker, like death milk. Savik no longer suckles my milk, and my breast does not produce more. He is living off of death.

Savik needs to kill Uncle, and he keeps pieces of him after he passes away. My uncle is forever in the makeup of Savik, trapped in his DNA. I hear Uncle's voice in Savik and see Uncle's expressions on his face. It's a small comfort knowing that he is still alive somehow, but it is also a Small Murder.

Father is falling ill. Now that Uncle is gone Savik has moved in for Father; my wonderful father, my steadfast father. His lungs fill with phlegm. His denim coveralls begin to become loose. His eyes betray fear and vulnerability. His palms beg forgiveness for his transgressions. He has always been good to me. He has always tried his best even when wrestling his own demons. He is a pillar. He has guided us children with a firm hand and hearty guffaws. He has supported and provided, gutting animals and scaring off predators. I cannot let this happen. There is no way I will stand by and knowingly let my father die.

In total despair I watch him getting worse. Savik is stronger now and does not even need to be in my father's arms for the sickness take hold. I watch Savik send the sickness to him from across the room. My father can be negative, so I am unsurprised that Savik has targeted him. My uncle was already ill so he was easy prey. Savik was still weak and

169

SPLIT TOOTH

learning his ways, so my uncle was perfect for the first kill. When creatures are hunting, they take what they can get: the old, the sick, the young, the vulnerable. Nature has no mercy. Savik senses that my father does not love himself and carries negativity; this is a perfect doorway for illness.

I try my best to shield my father by having him hold Naja, but Savik unravels the healing Naja weaves. It's time to leave this house before more of my family gets harmed.

After a Greatly Contrived Emotional Outburst Resulting In A Family Argument, I show up at Helen's on a Thursday. It's better to break my parents' hearts than live with them and watch Father grow ill. I needed the argument to be believable, so I asked the babies to give me Tears. Helen allows me to move in even though she can smell the lie. Best Boy moves in on Friday. Helen makes tea and bannock. She sings a song that silences the turmoil. There is a deck of cards on the table. We play. I sleep well for the first time since never.

The dream tonight is that a large salivating spider is on my chest. I throw it off in desperation only to discover that I had thrown Savik in the waking world. At the last second before he is launched off the bed I catch him and cradle him to my chest. My Small Murderer, I love him so. He is everything that is flawed. He cannot help himself. We all give ourselves to people that cannot help themselves. How can we not?

Life holds hands with itself

Because it is familial

Death can hold hands with life

But we recoil

The dead can speak

We try not to listen

Matter congregates

And creates density

Pressure is time

The more dense matter is

The more time it possesses

Owns more time

Takes more time

Life is breath Life is death

Time carries Life

But Life carries Time

We want to be linear

Entrapped in our vulgar forms

Desperate to comprehend what

Cannot be grasped

Because our marrow told us so

The dead love us

The dead laugh

We try not to hear

They do not need time

So we fear them
The dead hold the answers
But we do not ask them
For soon we will all Know

Watching Best Boy sleep is wondrous to me, and he has
begun to glow again. He leaves and comes as he pleases.
He likes that I don't mind. He is so brown, so smooth. He
has a quarter-sized mole on his left shoulder blade. He wears
threadbare T-shirts and scuffed shoes. He is always in a ball
cap. There is a slight rusty pitch in his voice. His feet hang
off the bottom of the bed. He twitches periodically. He is
dreaming of sulphur and pitch. I go and inhale his exhalations
just to see what will happen and the warmth stirs in my belly.
His mouth is slightly agape. He licks his lips in his sleep. No
one is immune to tenderness.

I place my hands on his kneecaps and absorb the knee
pain that has been bothering him since he fell playing basket-
ball. I throw the pain away and accidentally send it to a girl
I dislike from school. School must resume sometime. I might
as well pave my way. I may as well be powerful.

Back in my room Naja is awake and aware. She knows I am
impure. It hurts her to see my pettiness. Everything breaks her.

She eyes me with suspicion. I want her to be older and more controlled just as I wish that Savik were not a murderer. We cannot always be what we wish to be. I cannot be perfect for my children. These twins have lived many times, intertwining in echoes over and over. Isn't it time to heal the cycle?

Over the next few blissful weeks, Best Boy begins to become ill while my father has recovered. It's a very slow illness, almost imperceptible. Best Boy is young and healthy, so it is a greater challenge for Savik to bring him down. I notice the smallest hunch in his back, tiny sadnesses entering his mind. His hair is falling out more than it normally does. His nails are brittle. Naja and I have grown to love him. Savik accepts him, Savik even cares for him, but his death is still inevitable.

I want to stay with Best Boy. I want him to feel warmth instead of fear. I want to be loved instead of forcefully taken, to feel clean instead of invaded. I am feeling the urge to give my body to Best Boy, to join with him in unison. The Northern Lights filled me but I need to know tenderness.

Best Boy puts his hands on me and it relaxes my muscles and slows my breathing. I must protect him. Savik knows my side-eyed glances. Savik senses I have let the divide grow between us but he cannot deny his predatory nature. My abandonment only feeds his ire.

Consequently, Naja develops sadness inside her heart, and it dims her brightness. This sadness affects her healing power.

Good thing we have Helen. Naja is very satisfied healing Helen. Helen is old and has many ailments and generous love. Both are in their glory. Helen with her long flower-patterned muumuus and Naja with her sunny onesies, cuddling and cooing from day to night. They shine. Savik preys on men, so Helen is safe for now, although I feel she would become the next target if Best Boy perished. My heart grows weak and dark with desperation to protect Best Boy and torn with motherly love for Savik. If only I could help Savik, guide him. If only healing would become the way of the world.

Human nature is undeniable and kindness cannot be contrived, mimicked convincingly, or bought. We are what we are, and within all the facets of Being it is through the acceptance of our monumental flaws that salvation lies. Unfortunately flaws can exacerbate themselves in some people; the darkness multiplies and overturns the balance and all is lost. Once you have killed someone, the pull to the spirit world can be strong, the path paved with power and fanatical compulsion. We have lost the ritual of cleansing your spirit after taking a life. I know that once you have eaten human flesh, you must live on the unforgiving tundra alone for a year to purge the urge for more. Savik's power exists because he has been born of my own evil, my own hunger, and our ancestors' hunger. Nature is not merciful. Neither is he. He just is. He exists in true form and is unapologetically all-consuming. I am cursed to watch all my loved ones pass away, eaten by my son. Eaten by his need for power. Eaten by his hunger for life. He is on a diet of souls.

Savik bit my breast this Thursday. He looked me in the eyes while breastfeeding and began to clamp down. I screamed and told him to stop but he kept going and he bit off the end of my nipple. The nurses said they have never seen anything like it. I knew then and there that there was no room for him on this earth. I knew he would only grow stronger and his prey would not only be restricted to the old or sick, to the malevolent or weak. I knew his prey would become Love.

When there is a cancer it must be cut out. It must be removed in order to maintain the well-being of the body as a whole. It is time. I realize that darkening his light will kick a leg out from the tripod that is our little family, but his power is not mine to control. It takes forty-eight hours to steel myself for the task. I let everyone love him. I held him while he slept. I begged forgiveness. Naja melted her flesh to him, sensing the stress. She released once she fell asleep. I wrap them in two fleece blankets, one with bears, one with wolves. I brush their hair with fifty strokes. I clip all their nails but the right thumb. I fill their bellybuttons, one with salt, one with ire. I kiss their eyelids twice each and lick the backs of their necks eight times. I rub the bottoms of their feet counter-clockwise thirty-three times. It is done.

Eat your morals

Your thoughts

Your sinew

Your pith

Peel off your skin

Your indignities

Your strengths

Your sheath

I am in you

then

You are in me

You are now me

We absorb your strength

We embrace your warmth

Eat your eyes

Your visions

Your goals

Your hunger

Drink your blood

Your breadth

Your mettle

Your fate

I am you now

My marrow

Your heart

My brain

Your meat

My meat

You're meat

I'm meat

It's a dark and cold night. The stars stare and the wind has gone home. I take the children out onto the sea ice, near a wide crack. These cracks usually occur around strong currents; it's the only way to keep the sea ice open, the only force that can scare away the freeze. The ocean: mother of movement, monumentally submersive. The currents: conduit for inevitability, keeper of secrets. The salt: coagulator of ideas, agent of impregnable stoicism.

It is so cold outside. The cold is slapping my exposed cheeks and hardening my resolve. Naja is in the back of my amoutik and Savik is cozy in a down bag suit.

I take Savik out of the bag and place him onto the frozen ice. He is afraid and confused. He cries out for my love. He cries out in agony. My heart is dying.

I put my hands around his little neck and begin to squeeze. Die, my darling.

His neck is so frail, so thin. His face grows red and his mewling conveys his utter heartbreak.

Then his eyes change. He is no longer confused. He is angry. I feel the warmth and pulse in him begin to strengthen. He is not soft anymore. His neck hardens into a solid, boneless mass and he can now breathe through his bellybutton. He builds a wall of protection around his heart and decides to retaliate.

His flesh starts to grow around my hands. My hands are burning, the bones in my hands are burning and there are a thousand boiling blisters where I am holding him. I let go of his neck out of desperation and see that he is mutating. He becomes a small seal and flops into the crack in the ice.

In our shared agony, I had not been paying attention to Naja. Naja has become cold in my amouti. Her heart stopped beating because she could not tolerate the pain of the conflict and the shock of the Arctic water transferred from her brother's body to hers. Little sweet baby is gone.

I take her out of my amoutik and slip her dead Self into the crack in the ice. She floats down into the water and I see Brother swim up to her. He absorbs her flesh and they are one. She is he and he is she. Finally they are whole and the longing for them is an emptiness that will never be filled. The seal looks up at me with love and hatred, death and life. It looks at me with the Knowing. Then the seal swims away. I have lost my children.

———

It's time for me to die now. There is no point living through this grief. There is no way to tolerate life now that I have forsaken my own flesh and blood.

The Northern Lights have been watching. They know. They knew. They have always known. I lie on the ice naked and beg to be taken. Please take me. Take me to the place where my body no longer owns me. Take me to the promises that were left in my flesh when you took me. Take me to the place where I will never be cold again, where I will never feel pain. Take me to where the vulgarity of my fluid and flesh will no longer disgrace my soul. I beg in song, beg in scream.

I beg through love, but I beg in vain.

The Northern Lights come down and observe me. They see with no eyes and I realize that I am not going with them. They look me in the soul with cold indifference.

Fear. Fear encompasses me. I cannot move. The weight of their gaze pins me to the ice. I cannot lift my arms. My breath grows shallow and I feel the cold making its way into my body. What is going to happen to me? The Northern Lights are watching. My ancestors have forsaken me. Why? They see the bottle of pills in my hand.

From a long dream ago, I realized that I took them myself, and that suicide blocks one's journey into the spirit world. The spirit must leave flesh at its own volition. To interrupt means that one has forsaken Time. Time is God. God is Dark Matter. Time is the driver of flesh. I realize only once my spirit is leaving that all those nights my bedroom door got opened taught me how to be numb, to shut off, to go to the Lonely Place. I was forced out of my body. I was forced to pretend I was a shadow. Those nights gave me the pain that has guided me to death.

What keeps you alive in crisis can kill you once you are free. One must not choose to die, though one must die anyway. My soul is separating from my body now. That sick prison of flesh I was previously stuck in now seeming like the most beautiful warm and sweet palace. I am being ripped out of my body by the cold. Hands and feet go first. Breech death. Extremities gone. I am being peeled out of my body. Layer by layer I leave, clinging desperately to what remains. The reverse birth causing the last agony. It is the most pain. It is a horror. I am cold and alone. WHERE ARE MY BABIES?

I don't want to leave. I want my life back. There is no help and there is no light as the reality of what I have given up sinks in. The pain is not gone. The regret is forever. I leave my body to search for Savik and Naja. I leave my body and hitch a ride with the wind. I am not a human now; I am only Lament. The wind is the only song. This is why the Arctic wind screams.

Ice in lung
Ice in Wind,
Life unsung

Milk Death
Split tooth
Sorrow marrow
Whispered truth

After my grandmother died, my mother would pray to her, asking if I was going to heaven or hell. She prayed so hard, she needed to know. She needed to know because she had always questioned my origins. Concerned for my soul, she wrung her hands and worried. Fear made her pray.

Bypassing my mother, Ananak came to me in a winter dream. It was set in my aunt's house in Resolute Bay. Christian hymns were playing in the background. I was hiding under the kitchen table. I could see my reflection in the chrome table legs. The plastic plating was peeling off in places and my face was distorted. I was an adolescent girl. Tiles were missing from the kitchen floor. A baby was crying in the other room. A dog howled. Laughter bounced off the walls.

There were three women sitting at the table. They were playing cards and smoking cigarettes. I could see their legs, their polyester pant legs. One of them was naked from the waist down. I spread her legs and buried my face in the warmth and comfort of her. She smelled like home and tasted like hope. Then another pair of legs appeared beside her. They were clad in a long white gown. A pair of soft hands (with all her fingers intact even though in real life my grandmother had lost her fingers in a winter freeze) gently grasped my head and moved it onto her lap, to rest, and ruminate. The smell of Halls and tobacco filled me. Her sweet voice started speaking to me in Inuktitut. It was my grandmother, whole, free from the giant weight of sadness that I witnessed her carrying when she was alive.

She told me I was going to hell, but I was not to be afraid. She told me I was going to hell, but for a reason. She showed me what my role was to be. It was dark in hell, except for this wall of fire that resembled a row of large flowers dancing. Beside each of these fire flowers were people. They were souls that held on to their physical likenesses. The souls were screaming, suffering with unthinkable pain. Hell was trying to wear down their souls, grind them down with agony. As the souls grew weak, they slumped and grew transparent. This took thousands of years. Eventually the soul succumbed, and it would drop backwards into a hole. Hell absorbed the soul from the hole, and hell's flame would grow stronger. To be extinguished and become part of hell was the very worst thing that could happen to a soul, a thousand times worse than the torture of the flames. Once a soul was eaten by hell it became part of the malevolent force of destruction and evil, causing malice and murder in the living world.

I recoiled in horror as I saw myself. I had no form. I was a floating white spectre. I was posing as a guard. I had to convince Evil that I was kin. I had to feign enjoyment in the pain. But really I was tending the line of souls, gracefully floating near the holes. When a soul was about to fall and die, I would spread myself over the hole to act as a net and catch the soul. I would then absorb the thousands of years of agony, feeling it all at once, and the soul would be revived. I was trying to stop hell from growing stronger. It was why I was made. I am to spend eternity hurting more than could possibly be comprehended, to work for heaven, for benevolence and love. My grandmother said only a few of us were ever allowed the glory and sacrifice of saving these souls. Only the strongest could survive the pain and the wrath of hell. Only the ones tainted with sin and evil could fool the devil at the gates of hell. Only the ones with the brightest hearts would not succumb to the agony. I was to be proud of the honour.

I woke up already hurting, and have been ever since.

Forgive them they say

Forgive those that have hurt you

Don't hang on to the past they say

You will only hurt yourself

The past has birthed the bricks that

Build my bones

The past divided all my cells

Into this muscle I flex

Into the skin that I've stretched

The past is the house of these breaths

I do not forgive and forget

I Protect and Prevent

Make them eat shame and repent

I forgive me

Protect me. I need help. I'm unravelling. I'm afraid. Fear is driving my flesh machine. I'm running blind. Adrenaline.

Forgive me. Forgive my tardiness, my hatred. Forgive my dark heart. Forgive my sickness. Forgive my soul.

Shelter me. Shelter me from myself. I am armed and dangerous. Bleeding.

Beat me. I deserve it. Blacken my eyes so they reflect what I see from the inside. Break my ribs. Kick me.

Kill me. End this. I am not brave enough to do it myself. All I have is numb.

Love me. There is still a child inside. The shaking rabbit.

Cleanse me. Wash the blood off. I am still working. I survive still. I am stronger now.

Worship me. I am boundless. I stood up. I am worthy.

Start again.

ACKNOWLEDGMENTS

Thank you to Penguin: to Nick Garrison, for all his help, and Nicole Winstanley, for believing in me in the first place.

Thanks to the Sixshooter Team: to Helen Britton and Shauna DeCartier, for pulling me out of the gutter.

Thanks to Jaime Fernandez, for his uncanny ability to see what my dreams look like.

Thanks to Julia Demcheson, for her translation, and to Laakkuluk Williamson-Bathory, for influencing my intonations on the audiobook.

And thanks especially to my entire family and extended family for bringing me into this world and keeping me on it. And lastly, thanks to my friends and lovers, who keep my imagination afloat.

TANYA TAGAQ is an improvisational performer,
avant-garde composer, and experimental recording artist
who won the 2014 Polaris Music Prize for her album
Animism, a work that disrupted the music world in Canada
and beyond with its powerfully original vision. While
the Polaris signaled an awakening to Tanya Tagaq's art
and messages, she has been touring and collaborating with
an elite international circle of artists for over a decade.
Tanya's most recent album, *Retribution*, was released in fall
2016. She is the author of the novel *Split Tooth*, which was
nominated for the Scotiabank Giller Prize and Amazon
Canada First Novel Award, and was named a best book
of the year by the *Toronto Star*, CBC, NPR, and the
Quill and Quire. The audiobook edition was a finalist
for the Audie Awards.

THIS BOOK WAS
MADE FOR TALKING

For discussion questions, news on
the latest Penguin Book Club picks
and to subscribe to our newsletter,
head over to **PenguinBookClub.com**